HONEYMOON FOR THREE

HONEYMOON FOR THREE

HONEYMOON SERIES, BOOK 2

LILY ZANTE

AUTHOR'S NOTE

'*Honeymoon for Three*' is the second book in the '*Honeymoon Series*'.

It tells the story of a bride jilted weeks before her Valentine's Day wedding. This is a five-part series based around the same couple.

I have also written a spin-off series called the '*Italian Summer Series*' which tells the stories of some of the minor characters who first appeared in the '*Honeymoon Series*'.

The timelines of both series are connected and you can find a recommended reading order here.

Honeymoon Series:

Honeymoon for One
Honeymoon for Three
Honeymoon Blues
Honeymoon Bliss
Baby Steps
Honeymoon Series (Books 1-3)

CHAPTER ONE

A slick sheen glistened all over Ava's naked body as she lay in bed, hot, sweaty and sated. She glanced over at Nico who lay asleep peacefully beside her. Just watching him sent her pulse racing.

He was beautiful. He had sought her out. And he was hers, for now. Whatever 'now' meant.

She had never expected to find herself in this situation: in bed with a man during her honeymoon. Not her solo honeymoon, for sure, and especially not with a man she had met only recently.

Yet even though she would never have entertained the idea of this happening, she could not deny having had wicked thoughts of Nico in the days before, right up until the end when she had fled the Casa Adriana, the hotel Nico's family owned, earlier than planned.

It had been one thing to have him rebuff her so coldly after their first, tender kiss. It had been quite another to find out, from a woman who obviously still loved him, that they had a child together. This was something that Nico had hidden from her completely.

Overcome by feelings of doubt and mistrust yet again, there was no way she could have stayed in Verona a moment longer.

Falling for the wrong man once was bad enough. She could not risk making the same mistake again.

But Nico had come after her. He knew he had a lot of explaining to do. Now that he had told her everything, she understood. The child wasn't his. Five years of accusations had plagued him and still he had said nothing. Then the paternity test had proved what he had known all along.

Her heart filled with warm love for this man who, until a few hours ago, she had been willing to turn her back on and never see again. Yet Nico was nothing like Connor.

No way. Connor was something else.

Her stomach clenched as memories of being dumped six weeks before her Valentine's Day wedding jumped back at her. Lying in her sumptuous bed at the Hotel Sant' Adelina in Venice, with the most gorgeous man beside her, softened the hurt a little.

This had been the whole point of coming to Italy on what would have been her honeymoon. She had come anyway, without the groom, needing time away to be by herself and to figure out, at the age of twenty-eight, what her future life direction would be.

Even though she had known for months that their relationship was floundering, when Connor ditched her, the pain had been raw. She'd still been in love with him, right through until the end. But maybe they would have ended up going their separate ways further down the line. It was better it had happened before she married him. Just as it was better that he had confessed about his one-night stand.

Feeling slightly cooler now, she wrapped the soft sheet around her and turned to her side to look at Nico. It was sometime in the afternoon, and they hadn't drawn the curtains when they had rushed in, desperate to feel each other in the flesh.

Golden light streamed in, casting a yellow haze everywhere and soaked Nico in a warm light. He slept so deeply, this beautiful, handsome man and she resisted the urge to run her hands over his face. But she could not resist letting her fingers dance lightly across his bare chest. He, too, lay on his side with his arm across her hip. She bent her head and kissed the big curve of his bicep, where it dipped slightly. Just the smell of him sent a warm fuzzy feeling through her body.

If things had gone according to plan, she would have been lying here with Connor. And now she had Nico instead.

He was everything that Connor was not and the stark difference between the two men in her recent love life was never more glaringly obvious to her than now.

A sudden clicking noise at the door jolted her. She flashed a glance over her shoulder, her eyes riveted as the doorknob turned. The hairs on the back of her neck bristled.

They had put out a 'Do Not Disturb' sign.

As she sat bolt upright in bed, her heart thumped wildly, and the figure of a man skulked into view.

"*Connor?*" She rubbed her eyes and blinked, then hugged the sheet closer to her chest. Beside her, Nico still lay asleep, completely oblivious to the intrusion.

Connor's gaze flew from Ava's face to the bare-chested man lying beside her. He slammed the door shut, set down his luggage and took a few steps toward her, his eyes swallowing up the intimate scene before him.

"What's this?" His voice was surprisingly calm, but he narrowed his eyes at her.

"What the *hell* are you doing here?" Her anger replaced embarrassment.

Now that he was no more than a foot away, she recoiled at his closeness, still paralyzed from the shock of seeing him, and having him see her in flagrante.

Not that she was doing anything wrong, technically. She was still single.

She watched Connor's gaze take in Nico's handsome face, his powerful bare chest, with its dusting of dark hairs. Connor's face reddened. It was perfectly obvious what she and this man had been up to.

"We're even now. Is that what this is about?" Not the words she was expecting to hear from him.

"We're *even*?" she snapped, incredulous. She wasn't sure what made her angrier, the fact that Nico could sleep like a baby despite the storm raging above his head, or the fact that Connor had the audacity to follow her to Venice and to turn up in her hotel room.

I thought I had closed this chapter of my life forever.

She was about to fling the sheet aside and bound out of bed before she remembered she was naked underneath.

It was hard to express anger while sitting in bed with no clothes on.

Nico stirred beside her; his arm still draped over her lower half as if he was claiming his territory. His slight movement caught Connor's eye. Outwardly he seemed calm, but Ava knew him too well. She knew that his unruffled exterior was only his corporate lawyer façade on display. As he flexed his fingers, Ava knew that inside he was anything but at ease.

"Yes," rasped Connor, looking at Nico who had only just opened his eyes. "We're even."

The sound of a man's voice in his hotel room shook Nico's

senses. He rubbed his eyes and sat up, placing his hand on Ava's arm.

"Who the hell are you?" he barked; his suspicious gaze hooked on Connor.

When Connor said nothing, Nico looked at Ava. "Ava?" But she had bunched her knees up and hugged them toward her, refusing to acknowledge his stare, or Connor's presence.

Connor held out his hand toward Nico, in a handshake gesture. "I'm her ex-fiancé, Connor Beachcroft. And you must be someone she picked up."

Nico slapped Connor's hand away. "Get out before I call security and have you thrown out," he growled. Connor backed away.

In all this Ava remained quiet, but her anger slowly bubbled away beneath the surface. Her mind was in chaos; confused thoughts married to disbelief.

What had possessed this man to fly across the Atlantic looking for her? Why now? Why at all? She needed answers but was not prepared to have a conversation with her ex while she and Nico were naked in bed.

"Go, Connor," she pleaded.

"We need to talk, Ava." Connor looked at her fixedly. She had never in a million years considered that he might come for her. She'd been broken when he'd dumped her and had done her best to continue with her life, putting on a brave face for the world when inside she was bruised and disappointed. Back then she'd waited and hoped he might want to talk and resolve matters and that perhaps he might even want to get back together again. But he hadn't even contacted her in the early days. It was as clear a sign as anything that things were over between them forever.

Now, after her whirlwind of a trip to Verona, and having met Nico, she felt as though she had been freed.

"There's nothing to talk about." Nico intervened; his powerfully built body naked as the sheet slipped even further below his waist. Connor's gaze wavered as he surveyed his opponent warily.

"This isn't about you," returned Connor quietly. "I'll be waiting downstairs, Ava. Just give me ten minutes. Please." He shot her a parting glance and walked toward the door slowly.

Nico had gotten up and put his boxers back on. He reached the door just as Connor did and let Connor take a good look at his powerful physique. He held the door wide open.

"Out, now." Nico's face darkened. He threw out Connor's luggage and locked the door behind him.

Ava sat motionless in bed, watching the standoff between the two men. They were like fighting cockerels, puffing their chests out and suspiciously assessing each other. She wished she had never set eyes on Connor again. The fact that he had walked in on her and Nico, invading the quiet tranquility of their world, had shattered her new peace.

Nico sat down beside her. "*That* was the shithead you were going to marry?" His hands tenderly grasped her arms, as he gently tried to unwrap them from around her knees.

The golden hue of their afternoon should have lifted her spirits, but she felt as if the world had ground to a halt. Energy seeped out of her body. "I don't know why he's here," she mumbled, more to herself, than to Nico.

He moved forward, slowly pushing her knees down and the sheet fell away, exposing her nakedness. He kissed her on the lips lightly. "It's obvious. He wants you back."

Ava hooked her arms around his neck and reeled him in closer to her. "He can dream on."

Nico rewarded her with a searing kiss that sent her senses out of control. She kissed him back deeply, needing him all over again.

Connor could wait.

CHAPTER TWO

An hour later, a flushed Ava and Nico walked into the lobby hand in hand.

Connor was having a heated conversation, bordering on an argument, with someone at the other end of his cell phone. His gaze rested briefly at the two of them, then landed on their held hands, before he looked away sharply and continued his condescending tirade.

"Is he always so argumentative?" Nico asked.

"He's a lawyer," replied Ava, as though that explained everything.

"He's an asshole."

She couldn't help but agree. She didn't want to be here, waiting for Connor, wasting precious time. She wanted to be outside with Nico, carefree and happy.

The sun was still bright, and the Grand Canal glittered. There would still be a slight chill in the air, but with Nico beside her, Ava knew the day would be perfect no matter what.

Her original plan, on waking this morning, had been to go for a long walk along the river before visiting the Guggenheim later in the afternoon. That had been her intention until the clerk at the hotel desk had given her Nico's gift. The beautiful, breathtaking Flamentagostini bracelet.

She had gone running after Nico, needing to thank him and to return the gift. It was impossible for her to accept something so expensive, yet the thought that he remembered, that he cared, touched her deeply. So, when she had found him, and thanked him, just earlier this morning, *everything* changed. It was all she had wanted—to know that he *did* care. Because towards the end she hadn't been sure anymore.

After their many mistakes, with him playing the part of a hotel driver only because she had mistakenly assumed him to be one, and with him not being sure of why she had come alone on her honeymoon, after all of that, their feelings for one another had still shone through. Was it love? Perhaps it was too early to give what they had a label.

Instead of spending time admiring works of art at the Guggenheim, she had spent the afternoon admiring Nico's body. And he had taken his slow, sweet time worshipping hers.

Until Connor had walked in on them.

Now they were both not only starving, but also wanting to be anywhere but here. The thought of lunch at Harry's Bar had her salivating, but she was brought back to reality as Connor bellowed more orders into the phone.

Even the clerk at the reception desk looked up startled. He caught sight of Ava and smiled. She held up her wrist to show him the Flamentagostini bracelet and he nodded his head in admiration.

It was the only thing Nico had let her wear in bed. The afternoon had been spontaneous and satisfying. Ava smiled in spite of herself.

"That's better." Nico tugged her towards him.

"What is?"

"Your smile."

"Ah," she said, "you don't know what I'm smiling about."

Nico moved to within earshot of her and whispered, "I can imagine, and you can show me later." His lips brushed her earlobe, igniting her senses. Maybe they could skip lunch and just have dinner, later?

She was about to make her newfound suggestion to him when Connor's commotion burst her bubble as surely as if she had been slapped.

She waited with rising frustration for him; she was used to waiting for him. It was something she had slipped into more and more toward the end of their relationship when he had become so driven, to the point of excluding everything else in his life and giving over his soul to the prestigious law firm. He finished his call abruptly and stood up.

Nico and Ava eyed him warily.

"I've been waiting over an hour for you." Her ex gave her a cold stare.

"And I'm on holiday," Ava shot back, her irritation getting the better of her.

"You were supposed to be on your honeymoon." Connor held his gaze steady as his eyes scanned her face for a reaction.

"Then I must thank you for saving her from such a sorry predicament," Nico snarled. Ava flinched. She had not planned on having this private conversation in front of Nico, even though he now knew her story. She still did not want to involve him in her sorry mess.

"Can we talk in private? Please, Ava. It's important." Just as suddenly the resentment was gone from Connor's voice. For a short moment she was taken back to a snapshot of their earlier dating days, when he had been so much gentler and softer.

"I'll be over at the desk if you need me." Nico's lips brushed against hers and his fingers fluttered lightly across her cheek, in full view of Connor. Ava resisted the urge to pull away. She was torn between falling fully into Nico's lips, with memories of his hard body against hers so fresh in her mind, and pulling away, under Connor's icy gaze.

Nico walked away without so much as acknowledging Connor and Ava found herself once more staring into the face of the man whose actions had driven her to escape Denver.

If Connor had not called the wedding off on New Year's Day, Ava would have been here at this hotel with Connor on this very day. In hindsight, she considered herself to have been saved from a fate worse than death.

Now, the same fate had reared its ugly head, and at a time when she had least expected him. To make matters worse, he had caught her in bed with a man who, until a week ago, had been a complete stranger. If the world seemed to have turned upside down from Connor's viewpoint, it was nothing short of weird for Ava.

Connor held out his arm, but Ava refused to take it. She walked past him instead and sat down on the single sofa.

"You wanted to talk? *Now?*" She was still furious with him for showing up at all. She sat stiffly. Try as she might, she could not relax, even though the big soft leathery sofa coaxed her body to flop backwards. With her back as straight as a rod and her legs crossed over, Ava clasped her hands tightly in a knot on her lap. "How did you manage to just walk into my hotel room?"

"It was our hotel room. You booked it for our honeymoon, remember? Then I find out you've gone ahead and taken the trip to Italy anyway."

The muscles in her body turned rigid. "And you thought you'd just come along and surprise me?"

He looked down at his feet, his face reddening. "I'm sorry. I shouldn't have just walked in. I could have scared you."

"You *did* scare me."

"I'm sorry. I didn't expect you to be with anyone."

"You assumed way too much if you thought I'd be pining over you and waiting for you to tell me you'd made a mistake. Why are you even *here*?"

Connor sat down on the sofa next to her. "I'm sorry for how things ended between us. I'm sorry for what I did to you, for the disgusting way I behaved. I'm sorry for a lot of things, Ava. I was a mess back then and to call you and tell you we were finished, that's low. I can't believe I behaved so despicably."

Ava remembered that day well. "It was low," she agreed. "Dumping me the way you did." He'd been a total bastard to her. 'You didn't even want to get together afterwards to talk things through."

Connor hung his head in shame. He looked up at her and seemed lost for words. As much as she wanted to put that time behind her, talking about it now brought the hurt back. "You'd left me alone on New Year's Eve, when I was ill, and you'd gone to a party! I waited for you. I thought you'd be back so we could see the New Year in together. I mean, Connor, we were getting married in six weeks' time."

Connor blanched, shook his head. "It's unforgiveable. I can't excuse my actions. What I did to you was beyond cruel."

"You called me from the party and instead of wishing me a 'Happy New Year' you announce that you can't go through with the wedding!" Reliving that moment brought all the memories back so sharply. She now found herself doubting her choices when it came to men, afraid of messing up big time as she had with Connor. She had to go slow and be extra cautious with Nico. Or at least try.

Connor shook his head in shame. "Slap me. I deserve it. I put you through so much. Please, please forgive me."

She looked at him with a mixture of confusion and exasperation. She wasn't sure what he wanted from her. But she knew she did not want him. She had found the start of something deeper, more fulfilling and healing, with Nico. She stared back at him helplessly because she felt nothing for him.

"I've been a complete idiot, Ava. I've hurt you, and I have no right to come here after you, not after what I did. I made a mistake. I'm sorry."

"It's fine. Really, Connor. It's all worked out in the end. I don't think you and I could have carried on much longer, even if we had gotten married. I couldn't see it then. I was so distracted by the glamour of the wedding that I didn't give myself a chance to sit and think why we no longer talked much. But it's done. We can move on. We *should* move on and not look back." She couldn't help but be totally honest with him.

Suddenly, her future looked so much clearer to her.

Connor's large, sad eyes touched her. "Don't do this, Ava. I've been a fool. I've been under so much pressure at work—"

"Don't blame your work for what happened! You cheated on me, remember? There were fundamental issues with our relationship. What's done is done." She felt so calm saying this to him. The anger she'd felt towards him had vanished. Nico had filled her heart with love, and she wanted only to bask in those feelings. She didn't want to dwell on her sorry past anymore.

"Is he special?" Connor looked around uneasily, shooting a look towards Nico.

She wasn't ready to talk to anyone about her feelings for Nico. They were still so new and shiny, and she wanted to keep them to herself for a little longer. If anything, Connor would be the last person she would be telling anything. "He's healing my hurt. I stopped trusting myself when it came to love. Not that I came here looking for love. I didn't. But he helped me." She had already said more than she had intended. Nico glanced her way briefly and she smiled back at him, her heart warming instantly.

She ran her fingers across her bracelet, feeling the metal ridges and the contrast of the smooth stones set all around it. Connor stared at the bracelet but said nothing.

"I'm sorry, Ava. I really am. I was an idiot. I don't know what I must do to convince you. I've been thinking about us for weeks." He leaned toward her, and she was thankful she was sitting on a single seater.

Ava backed away. "Us? There's no *us* anymore, Connor." She tried to be gentle as she told him but could not help staring across the lobby. She watched Nico talking to someone who looked to be the hotel manager.

Connor opened his mouth and she braced herself for another lengthy speech then, unwilling to suffer any more of him, she stood up decisively; being gentle didn't seem to be getting through to him. "It's over, Connor. I'm over you. You shouldn't have come here. Your being here is just a waste of your time. I'm getting on with my life now and you need to do the same."

He looked up at her aghast. "I'll do anything. Just tell me what I can do to make it better." Confusion rained down on his normally calm face, yet she knew he was fighting for composure. She could see him mulling things over, trying to find the right words. Even in a situation like this, rather than gush out hurried, incoherent words and turn into a blubbering, stammering wreck, Connor would prefer to leave things unsaid.

"You can go home."

His posture changed, as if he'd suddenly lost his spine. Her words had wounded him the way he had hurt her on New Year's Eve.

"Not without you." These were not the words she wanted to hear. But the thing that really got under her skin was his implication that somehow her staying here was not a choice for her to make.

She pondered the meaning of his words. *Not without you.* She laughed at him. It was a cruel laugh, full of derision. "What are you going to do? Kidnap me?" She got up and left him sitting alone.

She walked toward Nico, her eyes trained on his wide shoulders as he stood with his back to her. He was deep in conversation, but just the sight of his broad back sent warm tingles of excitement all over her body. His very manliness sent her heartbeat into pandemonium in a way Connor never had. It scared her and yet it thrilled her at the same time, this slow but sure addiction to him. It was in its early days yet, but it was an addiction all the same. Nico had a masculinity that was sensual and simmering and full of promise. She had sampled some of that earlier and now her body was primed for more.

All thoughts of Connor were already lost from her mind the moment she turned her back on him. She reached Nico and slipped her hands easily around his waist, before sliding her body into his back. It was a forward gesture for her, given that he was busy in conversation with someone. But she felt light and dizzy, and she was on vacation, after all.

Connor had battered her soul and she wanted to be set free.

At her touch, Nico laughed, a low, quiet laugh, knowing it was her, without needing to turn around. Her breasts hugged against his rock hard back and sent sizzling sensations deep in her belly.

Such a shame we're in the hotel lobby.

Nico covered her hands with his and half turned toward her. He muttered some words in Italian to the other man and turned to face her. "I could get used to this," he murmured. He studied her face carefully, as if he was looking for signs of hurt. His gaze flicked over her shoulder and fell on Connor.

"Are you okay?" He pulled his gaze back to Ava's face.

She nodded. "I'm not sure he's getting the message, though." She tipped her head forward and nestled comfortably in the crook of his neck. They held each other closely.

"Can we go someplace else? I need to get out of here." She made a determined effort to pull herself away from the comfort and security of Nico's body.

"Of course." He took her hand and led her out of the hotel. They walked past Connor, who still sat on the sofa where she had left him. He was now busy tapping into his Smartphone.

CHAPTER THREE

As they left the Hotel Sant' Adelina, Nico was desperate to get Ava away from that asshole ex-fiancé of hers.

Ever since he'd found out that Ava had been dumped by that dufus only weeks before her wedding, he'd wondered what sort of a man could do that to anyone. But, more than that, he wondered what sort of an asshole would do that to a woman like Ava.

Now he knew.

The man had also interrupted what had been the perfect afternoon. He had spent most of it making love with the woman who until this morning he'd believed was out of his reach.

Their time together had been passionate but all too brief, and he blamed that all on Connor Beachcroft. He had the guy down for a total jackass but at least now he could put a face to the name.

"Is there any place in particular you'd like to go?" Nico asked, trying to shake Ava out of her quietness. He wanted to ask her a million questions, but he knew that now was not the time.

Ava shook her head. "I needed to get some air. I was suffocating in there." They held hands as they walked, then Nico let go of her hand and slipped his arm around her shoulder, hugging her closer to him. They walked in silence for a while. He would let her have her solitude; he could see she needed to be alone with her thoughts. As did he.

His last-minute decision to come to Venice looking for her had turned out better than he had ever hoped. That is, until Connor had walked in on them. Nico hoped the image of Ava lying naked with him was burned deeply in Connor's mind. The man deserved no lesser pain.

While the outcome of Nico's excursion to Venice had far exceeded even his wildest dreams, he now wasn't sure what might happen next with Ava. She wasn't like the other women who fell at his feet. For a reason he could not explain, he felt a pull toward this woman, and he was drawn to her in a way he had never experienced with any woman before.

It surprised him, to the point that he didn't know what to hope for going forward. When she left Verona, they'd argued, but she'd taken a piece of his heart and he hadn't wanted their parting to be on bad terms.

His father would put it down to Nico chasing yet another woman that he couldn't resist, but he himself knew that this time it was different.

As a virile young man, he couldn't deny that he'd never had lustful thoughts about her, but he'd kept his distance, as much as he could.

When *she* had come running after *him* this morning, thanking him for the bracelet, it sparked a ray of hope inside him. Perhaps they both wanted the same thing.

Only Connor being here could now put a downer on the rest of their days in Venice.

There was no place for Connor in Ava's life anymore. She

had told him as much, and from what Nico could see, the man was an idiot anyway. What had she ever seen in him in the first place? If the man had any sense he'd know that there was only one direction for him to take now and that was to return to Denver.

And where would that leave him and Ava? Nico had not given matters much thought, beyond finding her and making up with her. He didn't want her to leave his life forever without him being able to tell her how much he wanted her to stay.

Now that they had crossed that hurdle, what next? What future lay ahead for them? More to the point—did Ava share any of these thoughts?

Would a woman who had just come out of a disastrous relationship even consider a new relationship? Was he being too hasty in his desire to be with her? The last thing he wanted was to scare her off. He had to be careful, but he also didn't have much time left with her.

What would it take to get her to stay a little longer?

They walked along the streets in silence, unknowingly following the Grand Canal as it snaked its way slowly through the heart of the city. The bustling streets, old and rustic, were granted a majestic backdrop of stunning architecture and mysterious, arterial passageways that broke off at many points along the way.

He hoped Ava would soon forget the misery that was Connor once she lost herself in the painting that was Venice. Most visitors here did. It was impossible to not get caught up in the splendor and breathtaking, picture-postcard beauty of the canals and quaint old buildings.

"Hungry?" he asked. She shook her head. He didn't care too much for food right now either, though he had been famished when he woke up. Nico didn't press her further.

Instead, he walked beside her quietly and allowed her the space she needed.

They crossed one of the small bridges when Ava suddenly stopped in the middle of it. She grasped the rails with both hands and looked out across the river; she seemed a million miles from him.

He rested his body against the railing. "Ava," he said gently, running his hands over hers. "Don't let him ruin your day. He might have tried to ruin the afternoon, but we can't let him get in the way of what's left." He rubbed his thumb over the soft skin on the back of her hand.

"Sorry." She took her eyes off the water and gazed at him. "It was the last thing I expected. The last of two things and they both happened one after the other. My head's still spinning."

He waited patiently, watching her, but saying nothing.

"Can you believe he has some crazy idea that I would actually take him back?"

"What did you tell him?" His insides knotted at the thought of her with Connor.

"That I've moved on." Ava moved towards him.

Nico slipped his arms around her waist, hugged her closer as relief swept over him. She looked at him, and his mind went into free fall as he stared back, losing himself in her eyes which was as blue as the ocean "What do you want?"

"I don't want him. I know that much. I'm so...*so angry* with him for coming here and ruining everything for me but I also feel a little sorry for him too. I wish him well. I just wish he would leave me alone." Her body tensed against his, but it wasn't for the same reasons as his. If she stayed melded to his chest any longer, he wouldn't be able to hide his desire for her.

"Don't," he cautioned, running his hands lightly up and

down her arms. "Don't let him get you all worked up. What was the second thing?"

She looked up at him blankly.

"You said there were two things that happened to you? What was the second thing?"

"Us. This afternoon. You know... " She blushed as she looked into his eyes, and he felt a passion stirring again.

"I didn't expect you to come after me. I thought once I left Verona, that would be it and I'd never see you again. But I missed you and thought of you, and I knew I had to put you behind me. I forced myself to enjoy what was left of my so-called vacation. It was what I had intended all along when I first arrived in Italy. I never imagined that I would meet someone like you. I had no wish to meet anyone, let alone to start feeling the way I do ..." She chewed her lower lip, her words igniting hope inside him. "I thought if I went to Venice I'd get some distance between us. I mean, I'm going back in a few days' time. I never expected you to find me. But now you have. And then we..." She cleared her throat. "I like being with you, Nico. You've helped me to heal."

"I'm glad I helped you." It was sweet music to his ears, and he wanted to hear more. She was starting to open up to him and he had to let her have her say.

"But to go from that, to having Connor turn up again in my life—has been a shock."

Nico took a hold of her wrists. "But you're here with me, now. Try not to think of him because it will only upset you more." He slid his hands up her arms slowly, before wrapping them around her waist once more. She was soft to hold, and she felt just right in his arms. He could get used to this. He wanted to get used to this. "We still have a few days left."

She ran her tongue along her lower lip, not realizing the

effect it was having on him. It only made him want her more, right there and then.

"I fly back to Denver on Friday. You could stay here with me, if you don't have to rush back to Verona."

"I don't," he replied quickly. "We can spend the whole time together. I'd like that." Her lips were too luscious to ignore, his pull toward them too great. He turned his face down, so that their noses touched. "And even then, you don't have to go home if you don't want to."

She glanced up sharply, and he caught her look of surprise. "Well, no, I don't."

"Then don't."

"Don't?"

"Not if you want to stay." He could almost see the words churning over in her mind and he didn't want to scare her off. He kept his hands around her waist. "Stay here for a little longer. You told me you needed to get away, and now that you're here, what's the rush in getting back? You said you can work from anywhere."

Ava pushed away, taking a small step back from him. She didn't seem to be completely against the idea. "I could stay, I guess, but..." she stammered, and he sensed her hesitation.

"I'd need to cancel my flight, I'm not sure if I've left it too late."

"Relax. I can take care of it."

"You seem to be able to take care of a lot of things."

He shrugged. "I'm in the hotel business, I have contacts. Why not use them?"

What was he asking her exactly? Was it too soon? One thing was certain: if she went away, the chances of him seeing her again were slim. Therefore it made sense to not let her go in the first place.

She wore a worried frown again. "What is it?"

"What would I do here?" she asked.

"You're on vacation!"

"That may be, but I also need to earn some money. I've been away long enough. I could find some more copywriting work, I guess, but I should focus on my online store. I mean, it's my big goal for this year, to make a living from that."

"You always sound so much happier when you talk about your online store."

She nodded her head thoughtfully.

"You liked Montova. You said there were so many new products at Andrea's warehouse that you could sell easily on your site. Why don't you take this time to source new products? Why not make your goal happen? It's in your hands. Why not turn your dream into a reality and work for yourself?"

"I *could* source more products from there," she mumbled to herself. He'd set off a light in her head. It wasn't just for his selfish reasons that he wanted her to stay. He genuinely did want her to do well at her own business. She lit up whenever she talked about it and he understood that feeling, because he'd started to experience the same, the more he worked at the hotel.

If Ava staying here meant she could do something to change her future, then it made so much more sense. It would be a good start for her, and he would do what he could to help her. "I'll be honest with you. I want you to stay for my own selfish reasons, too. I like having you around, Ms. Ramirez."

"I like being around you, too, Mr. Cazale." She moved toward him, closing the gap between them.

"You'll see," he said, trying to encourage her. "It will work out. With regards to Andrea, make sure you strike a good deal with her. She's very competitive and business minded," he warned.

"A couple of weeks are all I need," Ava replied decisively.

"Of course, a couple of weeks."

"I'll need to find another place to stay."

He waved away her concerns as easily as she aired them. "You can stay at the hotel as long as you want."

"I can't afford it, Nico," she said quietly.

Nico half chortled. "It would be crazy of you to pay when my family owns it."

She looked at him aghast. "I'm not accepting it if you won't allow me to pay."

"But there is no need. That would be silly."

"I can't be bought, Nico."

His mouth fell open. "I'm not buying you, Ava." He silenced her with a simple kiss on her lips.

But the way her face remained clouded over told him this was not a good idea. Ava was the type of woman who liked to pay her way. This was yet another thing that set her apart from the gold diggers who normally sought him out.

He thought quickly, wondering what options he could help her with. That she was now thinking about living arrangements was a good sign. For now, this would be enough for him. "We have several pensiones nearby. I assume you'd want to stay in Verona?"

"A pensione?" she mused. "I'd like that. A pensione would be better for me. More affordable. I love your beautiful hotel, but I need something practical if I'm to spend my time and hard-earned money on building up my business."

"You can do whatever suits you best, Ava. It's your choice. You could even stay with me, if you wanted to." Just as he suspected, this final option threw her into turmoil, but he felt he had to suggest it at least.

She opened her mouth and started to reel off a list of reasons why staying with him was not an option, which made him smile. He put up one of his hands to calm her down. "You don't have to. Though we do have many spare rooms for guests." He stopped just as quickly, knowing exactly what kinds of thoughts his last comment would have evoked in her. "Before you say anything, Ava, I have never asked anyone to stay at my home before. I live with my father, but it's a huge house. He lives on one floor and I live on another. You would not bump into him, in case that was something else you'd worry about."

Her cheeks turned pink. "You're being very presumptuous."

"No, no." Nico shook his head. "I'm just giving you options. I'm telling you I don't mind—"

"I'm sure you don't."

"It's your choice. You could stay with us, if you so wish, or you could stay at the pensione, or," said Nico, leaning in close to her, "you could go back home and we'd never see each other again. It's entirely up to you." The last thing he wanted was for her to feel as though he had cajoled her into a decision.

A flicker of concern etched across her features. He could almost read her thoughts.

"I'll stay," she said finally. "But I *will* pay my way. And I won't be here for too long. Two weeks at the most."

Nico relaxed. She would be around for another few weeks, the thought of it made him feel better already. Putting her up in one of the many pensiones owned by the Cazales around Verona was easy enough to do. He would suggest the beautiful Villa Sagranosa; it was in a large estate with a few buildings in a row, all of which belonged to the Cazale family. It would be perfect, not only for its proximity to his hotel, but because it was one of their best. In a quiet location, with a vast lawn, gated—and therefore safe—and bordered by vineyards.

Ava would love it. Maybe he assumed too much about the

two of them, but it would give them the total privacy he hoped she wanted as much as he did.

"How much would a pensione cost? Because I won't move in until you tell me."

"Of course," he sighed and gave her a price. He would let her have it for nothing, but she was a stubborn and independent woman and if it made her feel better about the whole situation to pay, he would have to give in. There was no way he could now offer her anything free of charge.

But he would have his way also. He didn't have to charge her full price either. She was starting out rebuilding her business, and whether she liked to think about it or not, it was going to cost money. Andrea's products were not cheap and shipping products to the US would cost money. He made a mental note to ensure that he sorted out the shipping for her because he had many contacts on that side of the business.

"All right then. I'll stay at the pensione." The decision was made. "Thank you," she added, almost as an afterthought.

For now, they had a couple more days in Venice. Nico touched his lips to hers and drank in her sweet smell. He finally had a chance at something. He didn't know if or whether they had a future. But with Ava staying on a little while longer, it was a start. In fact it was a very good start.

"Come on." He took her hand. "You must be hungry now. All this thinking and analyzing, it has made *me* hungry. Shall we go someplace to eat?" He knew of a very good restaurant nearby. In a place where every eatery was excellent, it was hard to stand out from the crowd.

CHAPTER FOUR

Their days in Venice ended up being like the honeymoon she'd never had. This time with a dream lover, to boot. Often, they would just follow the meandering paths, the labyrinth of canals and alleyways around the city, holding hands like star-crossed lovers. They reveled in the time and privacy they had together.

Nico knew Venice well and he delighted in taking her to places off the main island; other smaller islands where life was serene and unhurried compared to the constant buzz of life in Venice.

After that first shocking encounter with Connor, Ava never saw him again. She was apprehensive the next day when Nico insisted they go to see Torcello Island. She half-expected Connor to turn up. But he never did. And after a while, she forgot all about him.

Even though it took a long time to get to the island, the boat trip more than made up for it. Salt water sprayed her skin and hair and revitalized her spirits again.

They stopped off at the Cattedrale di Santa Maria Assunta and marveled at the Venetian Byzantine architecture, with its mosaics and marble. Later they ate seared sea scallops in a tiny restaurant overlooking the river, with the constant burping and guzzling noises of the vaporetti in the background.

They watched glass being blown like balloons at a glass factory near Murano, and then they visited Burano, with its colorful riot of houses, and saw women making lace.

One day he took her to La Guidecca, with its laid-back charm and antique old-world ambiance. Ava felt as though they had taken a step back in time, to a world where smartphones and Wi-Fi never existed. It was available, because Nico needed to be in daily contact with the outside world, and he always made sure he was abreast of developments back at the Casa Adriana, but this quaint little place had an appeal that was endearing.

Here they walked the entire length of the island and entered the Hotel Cipriani where the staff fussed over Nico, and tended to his every need. He seemed to know people wherever they went; being the son of a hotel magnate definitely had its advantages.

If the island had taken Ava's breath away, she was captivated by the majestic splendor of the Cipriani and its grounds. They spent hours walking around, kissing like teenagers on a first date amid the landscaped gardens. In the evening they ate lobster on the terrace overlooking the lagoon.

He showed her places that she would never have visited if she had been here alone, or with Connor.

The days meshed into one long, glorious and colorful cornucopia of sights and sounds and Ava was swept away in the dizzying giddiness of life and love with Nico in Venice.

Here, with just the two of them, it was sublime. She started to feel that she was on a honeymoon of sorts, or at least taking time away from life, and spending it with a man she had started to fall for.

Just as she was settling into a mode of happiness that was long overdue, their days in Venice came to an end and their "honeymoon" was over. It was time to head back.

Postponing her flight home had been the easy part. Telling her inquisitive mother she was staying here a bit longer, and then sounding vague about 'why', had been nothing short of difficult.

The truth was that she herself did not know how long she'd stay in Verona. Nico was always telling her not to worry about the living arrangements, though she sensed he was a little hurt that she was not staying with him.

Too much was happening too fast and she had to put a brake on things. As much as she was coming to love their days together, Ava knew she also needed time away from Nico. Their time together was sometimes so intense, so heightened, that it made her giddy just being beside him. Nico was so passionate, so into her that she was finding it hard to be cautious. With him she lost her inhibitions and discovered a more sensual part of herself she had never known existed.

It was a feeling she had never encountered before. And it frightened her a little.

She needed time at the pensione by herself to recover.

The breakup with Connor had caused her to doubt herself, and she did not trust her emotions when it came to men. She was already having a hard time coming to grips with the fact that she was now on vacation and having way too much sex with a man she had only met recently.

Ava Ramirez did not do these things. Sometimes, when they finally went to sleep, she would wonder if this was a rebound relationship. Which meant what they had shared was nothing more than rebound sex. Rona, her older, protective sister, would describe it as such. Though Ava had no intention of telling Rona anything.

Was this fling with Nico nothing more than a feel-good holiday romance, albeit intense and hotly passionate? Nico oozed more passion from his finger than Connor ever had at all.

Perhaps once they were back from the headiness of Venice, and Nico was busy with the hotel, the ordinariness of daily life would ground them both. She might get a better picture of how things could be.

She shook her head, Venice did crazy things to a person and getting her to consider a future with Nico was one of them.

Spending time with Nico was a bonus, but that wasn't the main reason she was extending her stay. Of course not.

She was staying longer because Andrea had the best products she had seen.

CHAPTER FIVE

Their return to the Casa Adriana in Verona late in the evening was permeated with a sense of sadness.

Ava was in trouble once again because of the intensity of her feelings for Nico; she couldn't stop herself from falling for him further if she tried.

At the reception desk, Nico's father was talking to Gina, their hard-working desk clerk. He turned and greeted the couple warmly as soon as he saw them.

Something about the quiet smile on his face made Ava feel comfortable around him. Nico had his father's dark looks and she imagined that in his older years Nico would look very similar to him. Both had those hypnotic dark eyes, the chiseled bone structure and the height. Nico's father commanded respect: it was in the way he carried himself whereas Nico was a younger, sexier version and his looks captivated women wherever he went. She had seen it many times and, although she didn't like the idea of it, she knew she had to get used to the fact.

"It's a pleasure to see you again, my dear." Edmondo held her gently around the arms and kissed her on each cheek. She smiled back meekly, unsure of how much he knew about the time she and Nico had spent together. Or the reason she was back.

"Nico tells me you will be staying with us a little longer, looking for some products for your store?"

"Yes, he was kind enough to take me to Montova. I found many beautiful things there that I know I can easily sell."

"Good. Take your time, don't rush. If you'll excuse me." He turned to Nico and they spoke in rapid Italian.

"Nice to see you again, Ms. Ramirez," said Gina, unable to hide the joy from her voice. "Will you be staying here again?"

Nico cleared his throat and turned away from his father, who had walked back into his office. "No, Gina. I'll take care of it."

Gina walked up beside him and grabbed the diary from his hand swiftly. "According to this you're still on your holiday. You start back tomorrow." She ignored his look of astonishment and typed away on the keyboard as if he was not there. Nico was at a loss for words.

Ava coughed back a smile. "You've been dismissed." She giggled.

She looked around her at the familiar lobby with its checked black and white marbled floor and the gleaming chandelier in the center. She had only been gone a matter of days, but now that she was back, it felt oddly familiar, as though she was coming home again. After the way in which she had left, she never imagined she would be back here— least of all with Nico.

It was strange how things had turned out for her. Now that she was back, it was time to look forward to building her future. Venice was a much-treasured memory to take back home.

Home.

She didn't like to think of home just yet. She was having the time of her life here for now and she was determined to enjoy the rest of it.

Now that he had been so casually dismissed from his own hotel, Nico walked Ava away from Gina's prying ears. She could tell from the way his mouth twisted that he wanted to say something but was holding back.

"Anything wrong?" she asked.

"I need to speak to my father. I won't be long. Do you mind waiting here for me?"

"No, take your time." She walked over to the far end, to a small seating area to the left of the hotel entrance. A snug of comfortable sofas appealed to her tired body. In between each sofa, orange glass lamps poured out warm, seductive lighting. The area begged her attendance and she plopped herself down, glad to have a couple minutes alone to collect her thoughts.

As comfortable as she felt at the Casa Adriana, there was no question about staying here. It was an expensive hotel, and she would never allow Nico to let her stay for free, or even at a reduced cost. She was beginning to feel a little unsettled and slightly out of sorts. Not knowing where she was staying, where her luggage would be going, made her tetchy.

Once Nico had finished, she would ask him to take her to the pensione. Ava knew all about the affordable self-contained little apartments that were cheaper to rent out than hotels. She would be able to afford this for a couple of weeks. It would include a kitchen, too, which meant she didn't need to eat out all the time. This alone would be a huge money saver.

She did not have Nico's wealth, inherited or otherwise, and she was not going to expect him to pay the whole time, even though, so far in the times they had been together, he had. She would not be bought, and she intended for him to see how independent she was.

Stepping back into Nico's everyday life felt awkward. She could tell he felt different, too. Gone was the softness and in its place, tension had slowly crept into his face again as he prepared to meet with his father.

Things between her and Nico felt a little uneasy, or perhaps she felt unsure, looking at things in the cold light of day, now that she was no longer under the spell of the warm pinks and purple hues of the night sky in Venice. It was as if they had come to the end of their little mini honeymoon.

But she had to be clear about this. What they'd shared wasn't a honeymoon. She wasn't deluded about what this was. It was strictly a holiday romance.

Who knew how long it would last?

Her cell phone rang out, breaking the silence of her thoughts, and as she reached for it, her heart flipped a little when she saw her mom's name on the screen.

Nico slipped through the main office door, behind the reception desk. It led to a small hallway with two doors facing each other. On the left was Nico's office, and directly opposite it was his father's.

He had kept in regular contact with his father and with the goings on in the hotel while he was in Venice, but he knew his father expected some sort of debriefing now that he was back. "You look tired, Papa."

Edmondo Cazale let out a sigh. "I'm tired. I'll make my way home." He smiled, setting off a crinkling of creases along his eyes and mouth. "Venice worked out well, I see." His father's lips settled into a line as he waited to hear Nico's version of events.

Nico shifted in his chair. "Yes." He coughed lightly, not meeting his father's eyes. "She's an amazing woman."

His father eyed him with interest, then picked at an imaginary bit of lint from the arm of his blazer. "She must be," he said graciously. "I've never known you to go to such lengths chasing after a woman before."

For all their earlier differences, and all the time he had been apart from his father while growing up, he now sensed that his father knew him better than Nico had at first thought. There wasn't much that he could hide from Edmondo. This 'thing' with Ava meant something to him and he wanted to get it off on the right start.

"Look, Papa. With my track record on women, I'm just as surprised by my actions. We parted on bad terms—all that mess with Silvia, the lies, the deception. I owed it to Ava to at least have her know that the week she spent here wasn't a total lie. There is something about her I like."

"There is a lot to like about her," his father agreed, affection shining in his eyes. Nico prayed his father wasn't having visions of gardening with his grandchildren. Even Nico hadn't thought that far ahead.

"Goodnight, Papa."

"Goodnight, Nico."

He left his father's office feeling a little better than when he had entered. Ava sat over in the corner on one of the sofas with her back to him and a phone to her ear. He walked over and waited patiently behind her.

"I don't know, Mom. Maybe in a few weeks' time. Don't worry. I can extend my ticket. Yes, I can work from here. I've met some nice people and I won't be lonely." She nodded, a couple of times, yes'd and no'd and uh-huh'd. "No! Nothing like that. Why would you say such a thing?" Her long, straight hair had fallen over her face and she tossed it out of the way, and that was when she caught sight of Nico. "Mom, this call is costing me a fortune. I have to go. Yes, of course I have a place to stay."

He waited for her to finish the conversation, discreetly busying himself with his cell phone while Ava placated her mom, at least that was what it sounded like to him.

She finally ended the call and stood up, wearily, with a sigh of relief. "My mom wants to know why I'm extending my visit."

He nodded his head. "You can't blame her. If I had a daughter, I'd want to know the same thing." Their gazes locked at the mention of something that far in the future, a future that could one day become a real possibility.

"Shall we go?" Nico took her arm and hugged her closer to him. A warm feeling stirred inside him. Although he had asked one of the hotel maids to ensure that the pensione was clean and ready for Ava, now that the time had come, he no longer wanted her to go there.

"Are you sure you don't want to spend a night here? It's late and we are here now. Or you could stay with me." It was worth a try. "Would you like your room here for one more night?" He broached the subject carefully, dancing around, seeing that she was feeling suddenly skittish. "Ava?"

But her attention rested on a point far beyond Nico's shoulders. She shook her head, her eyes widening.

"Ava? If it really makes you uncomfortable, I'll take you to the pensione now."

But she wasn't listening to him. She said the one word that sent blood rushing through his body.

"Connor?"

CHAPTER SIX

"There you are!" Connor's face beamed unnaturally as he stood next to a shell-shocked Nico.

With the two of them standing side by side, Ava couldn't help but notice they were complete opposites. They were similar in age, with Nico at thirty-two just a few years younger than Connor, but they were poles apart. How could she have fallen for two men who were so different?

Nico turned sharply, and she watched, motionless, as his gaze swept over the rather exuberant Connor. The man was making a habit of turning up in places where they least expected him.

"What are you doing here?" Ava regained some of her composure.

Connor barely batted an eye and turned to Nico instead. "We were supposed to have come here for *our* honeymoon."

"Thank goodness for Ava's sake you didn't," retorted Nico.

The insides of her stomach knotted as Ava watched the two men exchange idiotic pleasantries. Neither of them appeared to acknowledge her discomfort at being talked about as though she were not here. "Why *are* you *here*, Connor?"

He ignored her again and addressed Nico, conspiratorially. "I was hoping to woo her back and to get her to fall for my charms again, but I didn't really stand a chance, not when I found her in bed with you."

Nico's face darkened. "Watch your mouth."

"What?" Connor looked from Nico to Ava, then back to Nico again. "It's true, isn't it?"

At that point Nico laughed. "You expected Ava to come running back to you, did you?"

"Call me delusional." Connor wasn't being so light-hearted anymore.

"A fool might be more appropriate," suggested Nico.

"Connor, please, leave things be. You can't change anything now. Things between us wouldn't have worked out."

"No? And you think this will?" Connor shot back, his eyes darting to Nico. The movement was not lost on Nico.

Unable to comprehend that Connor was not only here in Italy, but had now followed her to Verona, Ava dropped back onto the sofa, her shoulders sagging as the day turned into a nightmare in front of her eyes.

How had he known she would be back in Verona?

"Why the hell can't you just leave me alone?" Her voice rose an octave, and she wasn't sure if it was because she wanted to break down and cry, or because she was confused. After a long day, and so many different scenes playing out, not least of all her decision to stay here, she was no longer sure she was doing the right thing at all.

The two men stopped talking, alarmed by her outburst.

Seeing Connor and Nico side by side right there in front of her was surreal. It was like staring at her past and...possibly her future?

Was Nico a part of her future?

She could see him watching her with a worried frown on his face. "If you'll excuse us." In an instant, he had dismissed Connor and, gently taking hold of Ava's hand, he led her away.

"Where are we going?" she asked, following him down a narrow, carpeted corridor on the second floor. Off to one side, in an alcove almost hidden from view, was a door.

"For tonight, you will have this." Nico opened the door, and Ava gasped in amazement. It was a huge room, decorated in warm yellows, with a large bed, a dresser and a cupboard. Opposite the bed was a desk, directly in front of a huge window.

Ava looked around and immediately felt at ease. She peeked out of the window at the beautiful gardens below. She had intended to go outside and take a walk but had never found the time, yet. Maybe now that she was staying a little longer, she would make time.

She needed to rest and she was too tired to argue with Nico about taking her to the pensione. Seeing Connor had knocked the wind right out of her.

"I'll arrange for your luggage to be brought here. Shall I leave you alone for a while, to get your thoughts together? I know it has come as a shock to see him here. Unfortunately, I can't throw him out."

Ava shook her head. The realization sunk in. Connor was staying here, too.

"How did he know I'd be coming back?"

"I don't know. He took a guess and got lucky. He knew about the Casa Adriana, didn't he? He saw us together and assumed the rest. Who knows?" Nico walked toward her, and she fell into his arms when he placed them protectively around her shoulders. He lifted her face up. "I don't want you to waste any more time worrying about him. I'll take you to the pensione tomorrow morning. Just tell me what time." He started to lean in for a kiss, but she stopped him.

"Stay the night with me," she pleaded, feeling a sudden urge to keep him by her side.

He looked concerned. "Are you sure you don't want to be alone?"

She shook her head. "Also promise me you won't do anything to Connor." She could only imagine his quick temper. Nico's face softened; he held her closer and ran his hand gently across her cheek.

"Don't worry. I'm not the mafia and I'm not about to do anything stupid. He's not worth it." He brought up her chin and gave her a lingering kiss on the lips, smashing all thoughts of Connor to pieces.

Falling onto the large, comfortable bed, they kicked their shoes off and sunk into one another. Ava felt at home here with Nico. Happy. She lay with her head against his shoulder.

"He followed us all the way from Venice." Her heart sank just thinking about it. But the proximity of Nico swamped her mind with naughty thoughts, a guarantee of how their night would turn out.

She moved her head back a little and stared up at him. "Why were you acting like his best friend all of a sudden?"

Nico chuckled. "I was as surprised as you to see him. Like you, I want to know why this man can't take no for an answer."

"That still doesn't explain why you were so nice to him."

Nico rolled to his side, and she felt his warm finger trace a line along her breastbone. "If the man is in my hotel, I have to be nice to him. As a guest, he hasn't done anything that would require me to call the police and have him thrown out, unfortunately. Believe me, there is nothing I would like more than to have him out of here. Away from you, from us."

Us. She flinched at his words. Nico was talking as though they had a long-term thing starting up, with a future at the end of it. She had to take things easy, be more careful. Otherwise, she could end up in another situation like before. "Will you take me to the pensione early tomorrow? I'll be ready by nine."

Nico bent his head down and left a smoldering kiss on her neck. "Whatever you say," he murmured. She knew now that his mind was not on Connor any longer.

He slowly undid the top button of her shirt and her heart sped up with excitement. Her back arched and the feel of his fingers along her naked skin started to drive her into a state of frenzy. Each time he opened a button he covered her skin with long, wet kisses, the kind of kisses that soon had her moaning.

"I could go back to my place tonight, if you need time to yourself," he teased, his breath short and quick, his voice raspy.

She wriggled down the mattress until her face was level with his and met his lips for a slow, lingering kiss. His eyes were half closed and she knew, because she could feel his excitement along her hip, that he had no intention of leaving her tonight.

She licked his lips and probed his tongue with hers. Now that he had completely spread open her shirt, she lay there in her maroon lace underwear, completely his for the taking.

CHAPTER SEVEN

Tori fought with her mother for control of the spoon.

"Let her have it, Rona. That's the only way she'll learn."

Elsa watched dubiously out of the corner of her eye. Rona was adamant on feeding the little one herself, but the baby, now nearly seven months old was having none of it. She grabbed the spoon as Rona moved it closer to her. The pureed orange butternut squash and sweet potato paste soon clung to her little fingers like sellotape. Tori stuck her hand into her mouth and smiled at her mom.

Elsa sat down at the table and smiled at her granddaughter sitting so cheerfully in her highchair. Her own daughter looked worn out. Streaks of orange goo painted her face like an excess of blush wrongly applied.

"I'm worried about Ava," said Elsa slowly.

Rona slapped down her spoon and wiped the baby's mouth.

"Shouldn't she have come back by now?" she asked absentmindedly. Tori smacked her mom's hand playfully when Rona put a tumbler to her mouth. Then she tried to wrench it from Rona's hand with the intention of drinking from it herself.

"Let her take it," Elsa coaxed.

"She'll spill it."

"It's a spill-free tumbler."

Rona gave in and sat back in her chair, admitting defeat. Tori slurped happily from the cup and dipped her fingers in her food.

Elsa sighed. "She says she's staying out there for a few more weeks."

"She said *what?*" Rona sat upright sharply. "What do you mean she's staying out there? What for?"

Worry wrinkled Elsa's brow. "I have a feeling she's met someone."

Rona scrubbed her face, spreading the glob of orange puree all over her cheek. Tori giggled loudly. "No! Stop that." Rona's voice was on edge as she wiped Tori's fingers clean. "She's just been dumped. Why the hell would she go and find another loser?" She shook her head and groaned in disbelief. "That girl is a walking magnet for attracting the wrong man every time."

Elsa couldn't disagree with Rona there. She'd always wondered if Connor was the right man for Ava, but she didn't like to hear of her younger daughter spoken of in that way. "I'm worried about her but maybe I'm just overreacting. Ava's not stupid. She might have met someone—*it could happen*—but I'm not sure. It's just a feeling I have. She's sensible enough to deal with things."

"Sensible?" Rona shook her head in disapproval. "A rebound holiday romance is the last thing she needs."

"I'm not sure she's—"

"I told her..." Rona vigorously scrubbed the high-table clean. "I told her to be wary of Italian men."

Elsa flinched at the way Rona spoke about her younger sister.

"Did she tell you when she'd be coming back?" Rona stopped scrubbing furiously and waited for her mother's answer. Elsa shook her head. "Then we have no option."

"No option?"

"Mom, someone will have to go and bring her back," cried Rona. "Who knows what she'll end up doing, in that frame of mind?"

Beyond being worried at Ava's decision to stay in Verona for the foreseeable future, Elsa had not really thought of such a plan. In fact, she wasn't one to interfere in her daughters' lives. But Rona's suggestion had struck a chord. She got up and placed a soft kiss on her granddaughter's head.

"Now that you mention it, it's not a bad idea." She moved over to the kitchen window and looked out, before changing the subject completely. "What time will Carlos be over for dinner tonight?"

"Seven." Rona rose and gathered the plastic Peppa Pig bowl of food from the highchair. "Of course, we'll have to go out with you, Mom."

"We?" Elsa turned to her daughter in surprise. But she quickly understood. Rona was worn out. Motherhood with a hyperactive baby had started to take its toll. Tori wasn't always going down for her afternoon nap either, and even though Rona had been similar as a child and Elsa had managed to cope, she knew that the motherhood Rona had read about in books was not the actual experience she was having of it.

Acknowledging her daughter's need for a break, she agreed. "That's a good idea. It'll be good for you to get away, and it'll be a lovely trip for Tori. We'll turn it into a family vacation, of sorts."

Rona's face brightened. She had taken maternity leave for the entire year. Carlos continued to work in his father's restaurant and would easily be able to get a couple of weeks off at such short notice.

"Are you sure Carlos would want to go to Italy with me and with Ava there? Wouldn't it be better to take a nice family vacation somewhere else, just the three of you?" Elsa asked. The idea of taking off by herself certainly appealed.

Obviously, the main reason was to see firsthand how Ava was doing, without causing too much of a stir. But she also knew that Rona would go in guns blazing. At least if she were there, she could help avoid the friction between her girls.

The other reason was that—now that she was retired—the idea of taking off and heading somewhere different was exciting.

Verona in Italy was somewhere different.

"Of course Carlos will come. Why wouldn't he?" Rona had her own ideas about Ava's latest romantic encounter and would think nothing of dragging Ava back.

"Maybe we're rushing things a little," said Elsa hesitantly, "Maybe Ava will be back in the next couple of weeks. Maybe I should just tell her what we were thinking of doing—"

"No, Mom. Don't. We'll surprise her. How else are you going to see what she's up to?"

"I don't like the idea of spying on your sister. That's not the reason why we're going."

"If you're worried about her, and if you tell her we're coming, she'll be prepared. Or she might come back."

"That's fine then; if she comes back there's no need to go," replied Elsa.

"She might go out again another time, especially if she's been silly enough to go and fall in love with some strange Italian man. Goodness knows how forward they can be. I wouldn't be surprised if she gave him her sob story the moment she arrived and he fell for her, sympathy and all. And now she thinks she's in love. Mamma mia!"

Elsa's heart was pounding. This little trip to Italy would have been perfect if only *she* were making it. With Rona, Tori and Carlos in tow, Ava would be horrified that the entire family had descended on her unannounced.

But Rona had already thought ahead. "Mom, we can fly out within the week. I can book tickets online; we have all the travel documents. Tori even has her own passport. We're set to go."

Elsa's shoulders dipped a little. She was suddenly uneasy about the whole idea. What if she'd gotten it all wrong? "I'm sure she's fine. Maybe we ought to leave it."

"No, we're going, and you're coming with us." Rona seemed to have her mind set.

And just like that, the Ramirez family had planned their trip to Verona.

CHAPTER EIGHT

Nico threw himself into work with a vengeance. He was busier than ever with the hotel. And he had a year left to prove himself.

His father was testing him and Nico more than rose to the challenge. Each milestone he reached was met with a small acknowledgement. Nico understood this. It couldn't have been any easier for the old man to have built up such an empire himself. His father had worked hard all his life and not for nothing did he own a group of eight Cazale hotels from Verona to Rome.

But, Nico often wondered, at what price? His father had lost out on family life; he hadn't been around much for Nico and his mother, and the hotel business had demanded and gotten all of his time. His mother had missed having a husband around to help and the absence of a father figure had its own set of problems. But Nico had found plenty of love and attention from his mother and grandmother, the two women with whom he'd spent his formative years,

He was always closest to his mother and when she died Nico realized the extent of his father's regrets. Regrets for the missed time he could not get back. When his mother fell ill, Nico sought solace in women and vices, which peaked to an all-time high around the time of her death. He had dealt with it by locking himself away, alone in his grief, spending days and nights sitting in his room, in the dark.

His mother's passing had given him cause to stop and think. He felt a need to prove himself and looked back on his partying life with irritation. Village life had insulated him from the vices of wealth, so that when he came to live in Verona just before his teenage years, he was ill prepared for the parasites who would leech onto him because he had money.

It didn't help that he was also devastatingly good-looking, and the girls had flocked to him in droves.

He'd had his fill of that kind of life.

His father had thought about selling the business, but Nico had managed to partially convince him not to. He still had more convincing to do, and he needed to produce more results. His father wanted to take things easy in his later years, and rightly so. His father deserved to enjoy the rest of his life; he'd created a legacy and Nico intended to keep that legacy going because otherwise, the years he and his mother had spent alone would mean nothing.

He scratched his face in irritation. He'd been sitting at his desk surrounded by financial data from all the Cazale hotels. The Casa Adriana was doing very well, but the other hotels were not performing as well as he knew they could. He could get them to be great performers, just like the Casa Adriana but they needed refurbishing and had to be brought up to the same standards as he had put in place here. There was still a lot to do.

But Nico also had other plans. Why stop at eight hotels?

There was a hotel along the eastern coast, near Riccione,

that had been on the market for more than a few months. The location was good. One of his trusted contacts had seen it and had recommended it to Nico. Inside was another matter though. The wiring was old, the décor was ramshackle, and the place had not been inhabited for more than a year. The current owner was struggling to find a buyer for the place. In a time when travel was so easy for many people and more and more destinations were opening all over Europe, another hotel on the seafront did not present an exciting, or viable business opportunity for many in the hotel business.

But Nico had seen the photos of the plot and he had been well briefed by his contact. He would have to take a look in person, to find out for sure, but so far he liked what he had seen and heard about the place. He had managed to increase visitor numbers to the Casa Adriana, and he was certain he could do the same here. Already in his mind's eye he could see the potential of this building. He knew what it could become, and he felt confident that he could make it a success.

Maybe he could get away, in the next few weeks, to take a proper look at it? He had to be careful, he had to get it right. If he considered buying it, a purchase of this size was something he had never done before. This was wading right out of his comfort zone. But to win big, needed big dreams and Nico knew in his heart what he wanted to achieve. Acquiring another hotel and increasing the number in the Cazale empire was part of his plan.

Could he, dare he, pull it off?

It was about starting something from scratch. He wasn't content to just maintain his father's hotels. He wanted to build up a few of his own. The more he worked in the business, the more passionately he was driven.

It was plain and simple; he wanted more.

He leafed through the hotel guest book, something he did

on a weekly basis, as well as looking online to read comments that guests had left. This morning as he flicked through the pages of the brown leather book and read through the handwritten scribbles of happy, contented visitors returning home, he smiled. Their hotel guests were noticing the little touches he had been adding over time.

If his father laughed at him for buying the best bed linen and bathroom toiletries, here was proof that this was money well spent. The best recommendations came not from big, fancy ads in the travel magazines, or even a review by a travel writer, but from recommendations from the very people who had stayed here. These people were his ambassadors. If he treated them right, made them happy and gave them a vacation experience that they would never forget, they would go on and tell everyone about this beautiful family-run hotel.

Just because the Cazale hotels had been doing well over time, did not mean that things would carry on like this forever. Not in a world where cheap last-minute hotel deals were the norm and customers could easily find out visitors' experiences by going online. Their hotels had to be better and provide the very best in service.

There was no need to sell off parts of their family business. He could take the helm; he just needed to show his father that he could. He needed to prove that he had shaken the playboy mantle. Up until recently, his father had always been reluctant to let him have full rein of the business.

Now with Ava in his life, even if only for a short while, Nico felt the hunger to achieve more. If he was driven before, he was more so now. He had returned from Venice recharged and happier than he had been in a long time.

Thoughts of the paternity test and Silvia had been long pushed to the back of his mind. Dreams of a better future and hopes of a more settled life had started to take form in his mind, leaving him open to possibilities he had never considered before.

One woman and a life together.

He had to temper his hopes for he had no idea what the future held. But now that he had tasted life with Ava, he wanted more. Letting her go was not an option. Getting her to stay longer had been a start in the right direction.

Things were good right now. He had arranged it so that each day a driver would take Ava to Montova where she spent time with Andrea looking at new products. In the evenings, they ate at the hotel and then returned to the pensione, where she worked for a few hours taking care of her business, and he worked on his. It was idyllic. They were happy and didn't need anything else. They had each other, for a little while longer.

He understood that she needed to believe she had extended her stay because of her business.

He needed to know that a part of her being here was because she wanted to be with him. It was something he still wasn't sure of.

Time had gone so fast that they only had a week left together.

Nico flicked through his mailbox, quickly cross-referencing with his diary. He needed a relatively free slot where there were no meetings scheduled and he could go away without too much trouble; two to three days should be enough.

CHAPTER NINE

Later that evening, after dinner, Nico and Ava walked through the hotel lobby and slammed straight into an ear-splitting shriek.

A second later, Connor's guffaw added to the mix. She hadn't seen him since that first night back in Verona.

"What is he playing at?" whispered Ava. There was something about the sight of Silvia's blond head of hair, and the way she blew out perfect rings of smoke from the cigarette that she held daintily between her fingers, that annoyed Ava.

She only saw Connor's back, but it was obvious from his posture that he was enchanted by the woman.

Nico grasped her hand more tightly. Their desire to tiptoe past unseen was unsuccessful.

"Nico, darling!" Silvia flashed her eyes at him and tipped the ash from her cigarette onto the ash tray. Nico's grip tightened until Ava wriggled it loose.

"Sorry," he growled. He barely acknowledged Silvia.

They paused briefly and Ava locked eyes with Connor who had turned around.

Since when had he hooked up with Silvia? The answer

was not too hard to come by. Silvia was always floating around the Casa Adriana.

If she was upset by the results of the paternity test, it was hard to tell, looking at her now. The results had proved that Alessa, Silvia's daughter, was not Nico's.

This woman was not one for hiding away under a rock. Ava didn't know her too well, but her feminine intuition had clued her in, and she understood what Silvia did not want to reveal: that she was a woman who still desperately wanted Nico.

But Ava no longer felt threatened by this woman. Not now that Nico had told her the truth about his short summer fling with Silvia. It had happened five years ago, as he struggled to come to terms with his mother's death. Silvia had used that opportunity to try to ensnare him. Ava remembered Silvia's smug face as she spewed up lies with the intention of hurting her. She had warned Ava to back off Nico because they had a child together, and she had hinted at something more. It had been the final straw for Ava, and the thing that had sent her running from Verona to Venice.

Nico ignored Silvia completely and turned his attention to Connor. "I hope you're enjoying your stay here. Gina tells me you'll be leaving next week?"

Was Nico keeping tabs on Connor's stay? Ever since Connor had shown up here he had not come looking for Ava once. Not that she had been around much.

"Who knows?" Connor hitched a smile as he gazed at Silvia. "I might be tempted to stay on."

Silvia leaned forward and tipped more ash from her cigarette. Ava watched Connor's eyes lap up the sight of Silvia's long legs. But when Silvia turned to look, it was only at Nico.

"Your ex-fiancée likes it here too, Connor." Silvia blew out another ring of smoke, forcing Connor to turn his attention to Ava.

"It's impossible to not like it here." He lifted the ashtray up for Silvia.

Ava rolled her eyes. "Shall we go?"

"*Ciao*," said Nico to neither of them. He pulled Ava beside him, and they rushed out of the door. He walked so fast that she struggled to keep up with him.

"I can't believe he's getting so friendly with Silvia."

"I can't believe he was your fiancé."

There was no answer Ava could make to that. They walked along the road, still hand in hand, enjoying the dusky night sky before it turned to total darkness. The pensione was only a short walk away and often, more out of habit than anything else, Nico reached for his car, but Ava stopped him. She always preferred to walk instead.

"Why do you think Connor is hanging around Silvia so much?" he asked suddenly. It made her wonder why he was still thinking about Connor.

"Why do you suppose she's still hanging around your hotel so much? I mean, I don't think she would even have bumped into Connor if she hadn't been practically living there."

"Is that a hint of jealousy in your voice?" Nico asked, surprised. "Because you have absolutely no reason to be jealous."

"I'm not jealous." But this wasn't completely true. The thought of Silvia hanging around for Nico disturbed her slightly. "Besides, I'm only here for a short while. There's no point in getting jealous when we have so little time left together." She wanted him to tell her to stay. She wanted to know how he felt about her, because she was getting in way above her head now. She had even started to think about staying here, as crazy as that thought was.

He remained quiet.

"I have to return at some point, Nico."

"Do you?"

"Don't I?" There was a hint of a question in her voice, before she quickly collected her thoughts together. "I can't stay here forever."

His face clouded over. "No, you can't stay here forever. I suppose you have to return home at some point." His words sounded cutting, suddenly, compared to the nice and easy conversation they had been having. "I suppose Connor will be rushing after you once you leave."

Ava felt the stark contrast in his manner and bristled at the sudden change in his countenance. "Maybe not. Maybe he'll end up staying here with his newfound Italian heiress."

Nico shrugged his shoulders nonchalantly. "He's more than welcome to her." He looked at Ava. "The two of them deserve each other."

They walked in silence for a while and had almost reached her pensione. Finally, Nico asked, "How was your day?"

Relieved to have something other than Connor to occupy her thoughts, Ava replied happily, "Wonderful. I found so many new things I can sell."

"Good." Nico sounded genuinely happy for her.

"Andrea suggested something to me that I'm not sure about. She said her cousin sells clothing for children and maybe I should take a look."

"It must be Natale. I know her. Her family is big in garment production."

"If she has a great line of baby and toddler clothes, that's something I would consider checking out. I know these would sell. Parents don't think twice about dressing up their little bundles in the best outfits money can buy."

"Then you should definitely pay her a visit."

"That's what I thought. I wasn't planning to expand to clothes, but having seen some pictures of these adorable outfits, maybe I should try to sell a few. The clothes are beautiful."

"You already have people looking for products, as you say. Why not sell them other things they might also like? I like your thinking, Ms. Ramirez." As if to push home the point further, he curled his arm around her waist and dragged her toward him, stopping momentarily on the pavement to give her a kiss that took her breath away.

"What was that for?" she asked, pausing for breath, surprised by his sudden spontaneous show of affection.

"Because." He rolled her away from him but still held onto her hand as they continued to walk.

"Because?" she asked, and then saw the gleam in his eye and the faint smile on his lips.

"Just because..." It was all he would say. Hearing Nico's words of encouragement convinced Ava she was making the right decision. She had spent most of last week looking at new products for babies and toddlers. She would tell Andrea she would like to look at the clothes in Natale's factory. Her heart missed a few beats at the realization that her stay would soon be over. Once she ordered the clothes, there would be no reason for her to stay on any longer. *Would there?*

The sudden thought of leaving Nico and parting ways hit her like a wall of bricks coming down. Hard. She could get used to living here. And this was not the first time the thought had come to her. It was finally happening; pieces of her life were starting to fall back into place. Like a messed-up Rubik's cube being put right, the compartments of her life were gently being ordered back into alignment. Sometimes she felt completely at home here, as if she truly belonged.

The feeling was both alien and comforting at the same time and it confused her. The feel of Nico's arm around her waist pulled her away from her reverie.

"What are you thinking?" He splayed his hands out around her side. She loved the feel of him on her body. Clothed or unclothed, it didn't matter; she was energized each time he touched her. It was yet another difference between Nico and Connor. "I'll have to book my flight soon." The words tumbled out of her mouth.

Nico's hands froze around her waist. "But then again," she added, seeing his disappointment, "I don't know how long it will take, sourcing the right baby clothes. And who knows? I might find something else to tempt me to stay."

"You never know," he said slowly, a smile spreading along his lips, "the things that might tempt you to stay." He squeezed his fingers gently along the curve of her waist. She looked up at him and his smile made her heart melt.

"How do you know I haven't already been tempted?"

"Oh, I know you've been tempted. And I know *who* has tempted you." His eyes shone in the darkening light.

"You do, do you?" replied Ava, shaking her head in exaggeration at his presumptuous words.

"Of course." He smiled wickedly.

She searched through her bag looking for the keys to the pensione, as he moved closer toward her and whispered in her ear, "Andrea. And her store."

"I never thought you would guess. You are so right. It is Andrea, as a matter of fact."

His mood suddenly became serious as he moved back. "You can stay at the pensione as long as you like, you know."

"I know." Unlocking the door, she pushed it open. He followed her in and closed the door behind him. Resting against it he pulled her toward him. "I love ... that you like it here."

She gazed up at him, surveying his lips, his eyes, and then his lips again. No need to figure out where this would end up. She could tell from the look in his eyes that he wanted to kiss her, but something was making him hold back.

"I love... that I love it here," she said softly, unable to move her gaze away from his lips. He seemed to be thinking about something, for he hadn't uttered a word. She continued, "But I don't want to rush into anything. You, me, us. Now Connor."

"Connor?" Nico coughed lightly. "You still have feelings for Connor?"

"No," she replied, then drew away, so he loosened his hold on her. "Not at all. But his turning up here makes me question what it was that I saw in him in the first place."

"You doubt yourself?" He followed her into the small living room, with its one couch and small wicker chair. She sat on the small wicker chair.

Could she, should she, dare she bare her soul to him and tell him the truth? "I don't want to make the same mistake again."

"And what's that?"

"Falling for the wrong guy, falling for someone who'll hurt me."

"I'll never hurt you."

She gave him a subtle smile before getting up and moving toward him. He pulled her down on his lap and she reached for his lips and kissed him gently.

"Do you think I'm a mistake?" Nico asked.

Now he had her. "No." And she meant it. Saying it out

loud, without thinking, she felt as though Nico was one of the best things to happen to her in a long time.

"We don't have to rush, Ava. We have all the time in the world," he murmured gently, before his lips lingered along her neck.

Maybe she would extend her stay here for a while longer.

CHAPTER TEN

Sitting in the backseat of the chauffeured car, Ava studied the images of plump, rosy-cheeked babies in Natale's clothing catalog and scrutinized each outfit carefully.

She and Nico had started to look through it a few nights ago, but in the end the catalog had ended up on the floor, landing spread-eagled on top of her silk underwear, the last in the telltale trail of clothing hastily discarded.

Even though she tried not to dwell too much on his former conquests, they no doubt had some bearing on why he was the most exciting lover she had ever known. Memories of that night quickly replaced images of the cherubic infants on the glossy pages between her fingers. She blushed and hoped that the driver could not see into her thoughts.

Nico would come over late on some nights because he had so much to do at the hotel, but he always spent the night at the pensione, with her. Maybe he had a change of clothes at the hotel, or he went home in the morning to shower and change, because each time she saw him he was dressed in another sharp suit.

How was it that their relationship had reached warp

speed? She let down the car window and gulped in the fresh air, letting it cool her quickly heating skin. She only had to think of him and her pulse would start racing.

She coughed, and stared down at the catalog, forcing herself to think of matters at hand. Andrea had arranged to meet her at Natale's factory this morning. Even with the idea of selling children's clothing, something she had never done before, she calculated she could maybe stretch out her time here by another couple of weeks, if that.

She had joked with Nico about extending her visit; she had wanted to see his reaction, to gauge his intent. She had hoped for more soothing words, but all he had said was that they had all the time in the world. Which wasn't true anyway.

She wanted confirmation, something, anything from him to tell her that she meant more than his usual one-night stands. She had nobody to ask about him and only his reputation—what some women said and the press reports—to go by. Neither of the two put her mind at rest.

He seemed more guarded about his feelings, preferring to hide them than to expose the real him. In Venice, he had been more at ease, more open, more receptive. And they had been the closest yet. She had become swept up in the sudden passion of it all, the unraveling of the real man behind the mask, and she could not hold back, not that she had tried too hard to resist him anyway.

Maybe he was more cautious when back in his familiar surroundings. His father's expectations and the demands of running the business took over. She knew this affected him more than he cared to admit.

She liked to think that Nico felt something deeper for her, too, but she was never quite sure of her footing. It kept her on edge, the mix of excitement and the unknown, all blended into one heady potent mix that she was becoming addicted to.

Staying on a little longer, even to source a line of clothing, something she would never have considered had it not been for Andrea's suggestion and Nico's encouragement, was the right thing to do.

She regretted being so hasty in telling her mother that she had met some nice people.

Why hadn't she kept her mouth shut?

While she had tried to keep it vague, she knew her mother was always good at reading between the lines. The fact that she'd mentioned anything about Nico gave her another indication of her feelings for the man.

Even in the short amount of time that they had known each other, it was starting to feel less like a holiday romance and more like the beginnings of something more solid, something that maybe could have foundations of much more. And the thought of that scared the living daylights out of her.

Natale had encouraged them to wander around the well-lit and spacious factory floor looking at the designs. There were rows of machinists on one side and long tables of fabric swatches at the other end.

With Andrea beside her, Ava had inspected the fabric and craftsmanship of the clothes and come away fascinated with what she had seen.

Andrea had a good eye for clothing and Ava appreciated the second opinion. She knew her customers and the sort of clothes they would like. But she didn't know Natale, and she needed to know that the fabrics were top quality and that there would be a good line of distribution.

The two women sat at a table, Ava with a notebook and

calculator by her side, making notes in her leather-bound folder as she looked through the catalog.

"If I'm not careful, I'll end up buying everything again." Ava tapped away on her calculator. Too much, she had to pare back on her stock. Gut instinct told her she had a winner, but she needed solid proof first. It would be better to buy less for a trial first.

"Don't go too crazy, Ava." Andrea swept her thick dark curls away from her face and out of the way. "You don't know yet if these will sell. You can always come back and order more later."

"I know." Ava scribbled down notes and still tapped away on her calculator, before putting down her pen. "I *could* come back here regularly, couldn't I?"

"Of course. You could become that international jet-setting businesswoman that we both dream of becoming."

Ava laughed. She liked the idea of that. If she regularly placed orders and sought out new products, not only from Andrea's store, but other places and parts of Italy too, as Nico had suggested, she would always have a reason to come to Italy. And visit Nico, too.

"Coming here wasn't so bad after all, was it?" Andrea asked.

"It has turned out to be one of the best things to happen to me." Ava meant every word. Over the course of her time here, the two women had become close, and their friendship had blossomed. Ava enjoyed talking to Andrea and they bounced ideas off one another, both being business-minded women who wanted to succeed. Being in the same market, supplying baby and children's products, further cemented their bond.

Andrea was a good listener and Ava, who'd had nobody to open up to, found a good friend in her. Though Ava didn't divulge much about herself, she had mentioned briefly about the jilted wedding and her desire to come to Italy to find herself again.

"Focusing on your business has done wonders. You've got a real glow about you lately."

"Thanks." Ava didn't want to reveal too much about her recent glow.

Andrea got up and walked over to the new racks of clothing that Natale had brought in.

"What do you think of this?" She held up a puffy meringue type dress for Ava to see.

Ava shook her head in horror. "Too stiff and too ugly." She got up and walked over, shuffling through the clothes rack quickly and pushing clothes out of the way. Finally, she stopped and held up a pretty little lemon yellow frock dress. "See, this is nicer, don't you think?"

It was made from cotton, a lighter material and much better for baby skin.

Andrea agreed ecstatically. "Yes, yes, yes." She reached forward and touched the pale-yellow cotton. "It's very soft, too."

"And simple." Attached to it was a photograph showing a toddler wearing the dress. "This little baby would look cute dressed in a plastic trash bag." Ava gazed longingly at the baby's fat little cheeks and big, brown eyes.

"You would like to have babies some day? You would make a good mother," her friend commented. Ava had told Andrea plenty about her niece Tori.

Ava looked up from the cute baby picture in lemon cotton and nodded her head. "Someday. Not yet, I'm not ready."

"You have to find the right man first, no?"

Ava nodded her head in agreement and felt the urge to share her news about Nico. It was the only thing she had not shared.

Andrea squeezed her friend's arm gently. "Who knows? You might end up meeting a handsome Italian man. You look happy, and you look good when you are happy. It suits you. You looked so sad the first time you came here with Nico."

Ava's heart fluttered at the mention of Nico's name. "It was one of the best things Nico did, bringing me to Montova and introducing me to you."

Andrea continued. "He's a very good, business-minded man. He must have seen that you had a passion for business. It doesn't surprise me, him offering to help you."

"He helped me more than he should have." It was just on the tip of Ava's tongue, to reveal her newfound love interest. She felt the heady flush of excitement in her stomach in anticipation of telling her friend about her newly blossoming love affair.

"Be careful, Ava. Nico is the last man you'd want to get involved with. He'll break your heart, as he did mine." Andrea held out a white two-piece sleeveless top and trouser suit.

Her eyes met Ava's. "You and Nico?" Ava's voice faltered. She didn't want to know anymore, but her curiosity got the better of her.

Andrea stared down at her hands. "He was, he *is* enchanting and he's charming and sexy, too. But he's as dangerous as hell. I was very much in love with him. Who wasn't? But Nico is not a one-woman man. We weren't together long. He broke my heart."

Ava's heart crashed to the floor.

Mistaking her shock for sympathy, Andrea waved her hand. "Don't worry, I'm over him now. It was a long time ago."

That doesn't make it any easier.

Andrea carried on rifling through the clothing with her back to Ava. But Ava had lost all interest in the clothes and leaned back on the table for support. Her legs wobbled and she gripped the table for fear that she might sink to the floor. "You say your ex-fiancé has come back, looking for you?" Andrea continued, not realizing that Ava's world had imploded.

"Hmmm? Oh, yes. He arrived a few weeks ago."

"I hope you told him to get lost."

Natale reappeared and beamed graciously at them both. Andrea spurted off something very fast in Italian and the only name that Ava caught was 'Nico.'

"You like these?" Natale turned to Ava graciously and pointed to the two racks of clothing she had brought out. Her eyes touched upon the scribbles of catalog numbers that Ava had made in her notebook.

"Yes." Ava forced a smile. Her enthusiasm had fast evaporated along with her warm and fuzzy feelings of love and happiness. "Your clothes are beautiful."

Natale smiled broadly. "I will leave you in peace, if you need anything, let me know, *si?*"

When Natale disappeared out of view, curiosity pricked Ava. "What were you two talking about in Italian?"

Andrea looked up, trying to remember. Ava pushed, and she didn't care how intrusive it looked. She needed to know, now more than ever. "What did you say about Nico?"

"Oh, that he had introduced you to me and that you had bought out most of my store." Andrea winked at Ava who felt slightly relieved. "Natale's sister was sort of engaged to Nico many years ago."

Sort of engaged?

"To Nico?" Surprise pushed Ava back a few steps. How many women had this man had exactly? She tried to laugh it off. "He seems to have dated most of the women around here." Her laugh was fake, but the knife that pierced her heart seemed all too real.

Andrea stared at her friend for the longest time and her face turned serious. Summoning up her best act yet, Ava said, "He's such a player, that man. I could see it a mile off. He actually makes Connor look like a half decent guy."

But Andrea didn't smile or laugh. Her eyes bore into Ava's face and she waited. Ava rolled her eyes. "Wait, you didn't think me and Nico?" She moved her hands as if to signify their togetherness. "Come on. What do you take me for? I've already had one disastrous relationship. Do you think I'm ready for another one?" But as she spoke, the truth of these words fell upon her with a thud. "What do you think of this white cotton two-piece suit?" she asked, pulling out another outfit and refusing to meet Andrea's eyes.

Her friend 'oohed' and 'aaahed' over it and the subject was closed. The women worked together for the rest of the afternoon, selecting more outfits than Ava needed. Later, they sat down with Natale and locked heads, negotiating prices and discounts for ten items of clothing in each style.

As long as Ava had her business hat on, she had tunnel vision for her business only. Any thoughts of Nico were quashed the minute they arose.

CHAPTER ELEVEN

Ava stared at her reflection in the mirror of the white tiled bathroom at the pensione.

Her arms were heavy. Putting her make up on was a drag. She didn't want to go out tonight, but Nico sounded so excited.

She didn't want to see him tonight. But how could she tell him?

He would be here soon enough. Her stomach lurched at the thought of spending the evening having dinner with him. Even worse, he had promised her he had a surprise planned. She didn't like surprises at the best of times, and he could not have picked a worse time to do this.

Andrea's words now rang in her ears on automatic playback. *Nico is not a one-woman man.* Those words had obliterated all her feelings for him.

A man never really could change his habits. She had deluded herself into thinking that he was going to transform into the perfect man for her.

After Connor she would be crazy to put herself through this emotional mess again. As loud and clear as she could hear

Andrea's warning bell in her head, Rona's warnings about hot-blooded Italian men also added to the clang in her head.

She applied her eyeliner, leaving a thin trail along the outside of her eyes. She got out her mascara, then put it away again. No need to make an effort. She huffed in annoyance. She wasn't prettying herself up for Nico, she was making herself look better. A dash of mascara made her feel better.

She ran her fingers through her hair and left it at that. Tonight, she would tell him.

There was no need to extend her trip any longer. Not now.

She had allowed herself to develop feelings for another man who would only hurt her. She promised herself she would never let that happen again.

As the quiet roar of Nico's engine reverberated outside, she rushed, grabbed her bag and darted out the door. She reached the car just as Nico turned the engine off.

He looked up in surprise as she climbed inside. She knew he had expected to come in, just as he always did.

She ignored the surge of electricity that charged through her as his fingers brushed hers. Even worse was seeing him in his dark designer suit. He looked like a man out of a cologne ad, the type that had a woman swooning over his chiseled features and bedroom eyes.

Her heart jolted. This wasn't going to be an easy evening. Not with him looking like he did. He wore his suits like a second skin and the beautifully cut black Italian suit showed off his tall and slim figure yet exaggerated his wide shoulders. Goddamn it, she cursed silently. In her desire to dress down, she now felt completely understated in her dark jeans and top.

"Should I have worn a dress or something?" she breathed, anxious to drag her gaze away from his oh-so-sexy body until her eyes met his dark, glittering ones. They were just as dangerous. Another stab of excitement tasered her heart. She was a goner. Nico was turning on his charm big time tonight. "I would rather have you in nothing," he answered, his wolfish smile spreading goosepimples all over her skin.

"I feel underdressed compared to you," she managed to say.

What was the occasion? She struggled to think about their last encounter and remembered, with a sinking feeling, that she had discussed with him the possibility of staying on longer. She had primed him to expect more.

And now she was going to have to let him down with a thud.

"You never look underdressed." His eyes raked over her outfit appreciatively. His face scrutinized hers as if he knew immediately that something was wrong. "We don't have to go out tonight, if you don't feel like it." His lips barely brushed hers.

Oh god, this man could flirt and tease.

She didn't want his lips to brush so lightly. She wanted his mouth to sink down on hers and for his tongue to claim hers the way he always did when his hunger always got the better of him. She wanted it, even though she should have known better; even though she knew she was just one of his many.

She pulled away. She couldn't give in now, even as she gazed a little too long at his lips, at the fullness of them, and took in the heady scent of his aftershave. She had to be strong and face reality. *This* was not going to work, no matter how much she liked to believe it might.

No, staying in tonight at her place with him was not an option at any cost. "Let's go. I want to go out. What is this surprise?"

His face registered surprise and confusion at her

reluctance to stay close to him, and he didn't follow through with the kiss that he had obviously intended.

He watched her carefully. "You'll see."

She knew from his short words, that her reluctance had changed his mood slightly.

They drove in silence. She had lost the heart to break into normal conversation with him, lest she lead him down the wrong path.

After a few minutes of strained silence, Nico turned on the radio.

"Andrea took me to Natale's factory."

"Ah, yes. You did say you were going there."

She waited for him to elaborate more, but Nico kept his eyes firmly on the road in front and said nothing.

After they had been driving for a while, he pulled up and the street looked familiar. She recognized the courtyard and the statue. They were back at the Casa di Giulietta.

"I didn't know that you had been engaged to Natale's sister."

"I've been engaged many times."

Not the answer she was expecting.

"Really?" her voice went up an octave, giving away her attempt to appear unaffected.

They had parked and Nico turned to her, apparently not willing to get out yet.

"Really." In the darkness of the car, his eyes sparkled. "It depends on who you listen to and what magazines you read."

"So, you *weren't* engaged?"

"Ava. There was no 'engagement,' not in a real sense of the word. Everyone assumed we were going to get engaged, but we were very young. It's a small-town mentality here. Other people and both our parents wanted to believe we would get together. She was a sweet girl. She still is, I assume. I don't know, I haven't seen her for a long time."

The hold on Ava's heart relaxed a little.

"Anything else?" he asked patiently, though the edge of weariness in his voice was not lost on her.

She hesitated; Andrea's words tip-toed on the tip of her tongue. She waited for him to tell her about Andrea. But he didn't say anything.

"I'm sorry if I sounded like I was being nosy. It's just that Natale and Andrea were talking about you. To me it seems as though you've dated all the women in Verona."

He let out a loud, audible sigh and gripped the steering wheel, his knuckles white.

"People talk all the time. What are you going to do? Listen to their gossip? Base your decisions about me on what you hear from idle mouths?"

"No, no...I..." Words escaped her. She felt foolish and thanked the stars that he couldn't see her face or the crimson shade she had become now that the tables were turned and he was the one accusing her.

"Do you still want to eat? Or shall I drive you home?"

She had made up her mind. She had no choice but to end it tonight. She needed to have this last dinner with him even though she had the feeling that she was going to regret it later.

"No, let's eat. I'm sorry. I don't want to ruin the evening." *Liar.* "And we need to talk."

These last words caught his attention. "Let's go, then."

He had walked over to her side to get her door, but she was already out. "You don't have to open my door for me all the time, Nico. I'm capable of doing it myself."

His hand brushed hers as she slammed the door shut. "I know you're capable. It's how I've been brought up. Don't read too much into it." He was standing so close to her that, had it been any other time, he would have reached out and touched her. But now he didn't move an inch.

As the subtle hint of his aftershave reached her, she felt her concerns ebbing away. The temptation to move her face closer to him was thwarted only by his aloofness. "Come," he said, taking her lightly by the hand. Gone was his usual tight, comforting grip as he led her toward Juliet's balcony. He exchanged friendly banter with a man who stood at the entrance before he moved past him.

"Isn't it closed now?"

"Not for us." He grinned at the look of disbelief on her face as he led her up the stairs. She had forgotten: this man had the contacts—and the money—to do what he wanted, whenever he wanted. It should not have come as a surprise to her that he could order the Casa di Giulietta to open at a time when it was closed to everyone else.

As she followed Nico into a large dimly lit room, she caught her breath at the sight of a beautifully dressed candlelit table for two, just in front of the balcony. The balcony doors had been pulled wide open revealing the backdrop of an inky night sky studded with stars as sparkly as diamonds.

Her heart leapt for joy before screeching to a sudden stop.

This made her mission harder.

"It's beautiful," she gasped. He guided her to the table and pulled out a chair for her. A blur of cream candles and brightly colored flowers dazzled her momentarily, but her heart was heavy. She sat down, trying to still her emotions. This was beautiful. But it was also too much. And it threw her mind into further confusion.

How was she supposed to end it now?

Nico poured her a glass of champagne and handed it to her, gingerly.

"You don't like it?" he asked, lowering his head.

"I-I-I..." What could she say? She was touched deeply by the effort he had gone to. But she was struggling to marry his actions with the words that rang ever louder in her ears.

Nico is not a one-woman man.

She was torn between which version of Nico was real. More than anything, she feared falling into another messy relationship. Her heart had already been fractured. Getting in deep with Nico spelled disaster.

He would hurt her. It was inevitable, no matter how he tried to explain his way out of it.

"It's beautiful. It really is." She waved her arm toward the table and the rest of the room. "You didn't have to do any of this, Nico."

What is it that you're trying to cover up?

"You really don't like it." He seemed downcast and left his glass of champagne on the table.

Now she really did feel awful.

"I don't need lavish displays of affection, Nico. I don't need to be wooed and wined and dined."

"I'm not doing it to win you over," he said quickly.

"So tell me, what are we celebrating?" She picked up his glass and gave it back to him, trying to make an effort to recover whatever was left of the evening.

Nico sat forward and raised his glass. "To better times for your business." He chinked his glass with hers and her heart dropped. He had only ever intended the best for her. "And because I remembered that when you first came to the Casa di Giulietta, you ran out in tears."

Ava swallowed hard. She remembered that time. It was the day after she had arrived in Verona. She had run crying from the Casa di Giulietta because a wedding was due to take place.

Nico continued, his dark brown eyes piercing into hers. "I wanted you to have happier memories of this place, to take away your sad ones."

She pressed a hand against her breastbone, her mouth opened but no words came out.

"I'm sorry if this seems like too much, over the top, me showing off. It wasn't my intention. I wanted things to be better for you. I feel as though things are slowly starting to change for you to happier times. I want this celebration to be something to mark the start of that time for you."

She placed her hand over his, not daring to meet his eyes. He placed his hand over hers and they sat there, bound together for a moment. Ava knew she had to tell him now.

Just as she opened her mouth, he said, "We can get a Panini from one of the kiosks, if you'd prefer that instead."

"No. I love this." She looked around her, still in awe at what he had planned for her. It was so perfect. The only thing wrong was the timing. She gulped her champagne down.

"Very well." He nodded, and it was only when Ava turned around that she saw a waiter standing discreetly at the far end of the room.

"I hope you won't mind, but I took the liberty of ordering for us, to keep things simple."

"Simple? You?" She mocked him, while holding her glass up for him to pour more champagne.

"Fish and lots of vegetables?"

She nodded excitedly. He knew her so well in the short time they had been together.

"And lots of champagne. I know."

She giggled more from relief that the atmosphere had lightened a little. Needing strength quickly, and before the drink made her forget why, she took another big gulp from her glass.

It would be so easy to let this evening roll along as blissfully as it was turning out, but her stomach churned. He had explained away the engagement, but he hadn't mentioned Andrea. He must have known that she and Andrea had become good friends by now, sharing all sorts of secrets and news. He knew she spent most of her time in Montova. Did she have to pry every piece of information out of him? Would he never willingly offer up any news himself? What was he hiding? Did he hope that if she didn't ask, she did not know, and therefore there was no need to tell her?

Just like Connor and the woman at the law seminar.

Judging by the way the evening was going, and Nico's expectations along with it, things would only get worse the longer she kept it all to herself.

"Andrea tells me that you've almost bought out her entire store."

When did he talk to Andrea? How often did they call each other? She guzzled more champagne.

"You love this champagne?" He summoned the waiter to get another bottle.

Great, thought Ava, *I'm going to need it.*

Courage spilled over. "How do you know? I didn't realize Andrea kept you so well updated." The accusation hung in the air like a dank stench.

"Of course we still talk. Why wouldn't we?"

She wondered what else he still did with Andrea. She had drunk almost three glasses of champagne and she was in no mood to figure out what made sense or did not. It seemed that at every point along their relationship, news of another woman from his past wafted through into her present.

She could not compete, not with these many women. Who knew what other secrets would be uncovered the further she travelled along with him?

"I didn't know that you and Andrea had a ...thing... a few years ago. You never mentioned it to me."

His face didn't hide the surprise. "It's not a secret and there is nothing to hide. It happened just after my mother passed away. After Silvia, if you really want the timeline. I didn't think it was pertinent to tell you." His explanation did nothing to pacify her.

"And you still talk to her? You spoke about me? Are you using her to get to know me better?"

His features darkened along with the mood in the room.

"We're still good friends. We still care about each other. I know it sounds to you as though I have bedded every woman in Verona—"

"Haven't you?" she sniped, then regretted her remark immediately. She was beginning to sound more and more like a bitch and that was not her intention.

"No. I haven't. And no, I didn't use Andrea to get to know you better. I can get to know you better by myself. I took you to Montova and you liked what she sold. You decided to buy more from her and get more involved. All I have ever done is to support you."

She hated that everything she said made her seem so ungrateful. The truth of it was that each time she felt closer to Nico and their relationship started to move forward, towards something deeper, news of another woman and another conquest would worm itself out of the woodwork. She didn't want to spend her life wondering what would come next. She shuddered to think that lurking out there might be another Silvia and Alessa, a woman spurned and another child he would have to prove he hadn't fathered.

She couldn't deal with his past, nor did she have the strength to want to try.

"Nico, I'm going back home. I'm done with everything

here." She banged down her champagne glass and ran her fingers delicately around the rim of the Murano glass vase in the middle of the table.

"I see," was all that he said.

Two waiters arrived carrying large silver domes, which they placed before them and lifted the lids off.

"Thank you," murmured Ava, trying her best to summon up the enthusiasm that had just escaped her body, leaving her like a deflated balloon.

"*Grazie*," growled Nico. He looked like a man who had not only lost his appetite for food, but for life as well.

They faced each other across the table, curls of steam spiraled upwards from colorfully arranged food laid out on huge white porcelain plates. Food that looked so pretty it seemed a shame to eat it. The aroma of lightly sautéed vegetables and fresh fish baked in olive oil made her mouth water. The guilt piled on.

How could she even think about food at a time like this?

She looked at Nico, his eyes downcast and his fingers resting on the edge of the table. Even when he looked down, he had the most beautiful face. Chiseled, with a firm jaw line, and the perfect nose. And a mouth that was made for hours of kissing.

His jaw clenched and she knew he held back from saying something that he wanted.

"We should eat," he said finally, picking up his fork. "It's getting late."

The conversation had died long before they had even arrived here.

CHAPTER TWELVE

He dropped Ava at the pensione and returned to the Casa Adriana.

It would be the first time since their return from Venice that they would not be spending the night together.

It was late enough to go home, but Nico knew he would not be able to sleep. He sat at his desk with his elbows resting on the table and let his head fall forward into his hands.

This was not the way this evening was supposed to end. Out of nowhere Ava had hit him with the news of her imminent return home. It was only a few days ago that she had mentioned the possibility of staying longer.

He had allowed himself to believe that Ava's feelings for him were growing stronger. He sensed that she was cautious, and he'd tried to play it cool, not getting too enthusiastic when she mentioned she might prolong her stay.

What had gone wrong so quickly? It couldn't have been idle gossip about him dating Natale's sister, could it? Or Andrea? That was a long time ago.

He lifted his head up and sat back, his shoulders drooping. He tapped a pen absent- mindedly on the desk.

Tap-tap-tap-tap-tap.

The noise was a welcome relief to him, if only to remind him that he was alive and breathing. His body felt lifeless, and it was all because of this one woman.

No other woman had ever gotten under his skin. Women flocked to him, and once they did, they never left. *He* had always been the one to ditch *them*. For all his life, he had been the man who could pick and choose partners at whim. In his younger years he'd been caught up in the headiness of the wealthy circles he moved in—where there was an abundance of beautiful women all too eager to drop their panties at his command.

He might have been a good-looking rich businessman's son, but he wasn't naïve to the point of being stupid. He knew exactly why he was so popular with everyone, not just the women. He was the rich kid and people liked to make connections with him.

But it had all started to wane ever since his mother had fallen ill.

Casual relationships ceased to hold any allure for him once his beloved mother lay dying. He had never felt as helpless as he had when there'd been nothing he or his father could do to help her live.

No amount of money in the world could make her well again.

The stark reality of life—vulnerable, unpredictable and out of his control—hit him.

When his mother died, his world shattered, and no amount of sex and debauchery could save him or make him forget.

Though he had barely tolerated Silvia when they were younger, she was one of the few of his rich friends that came to his aid. She had not been scared off by the tragedy of his mother's illness and in his grief, he had allowed himself to get close to her. Somehow, she had wormed her way into his life and witnessed firsthand his bare, broken soul.

He had needed her, and she had helped him. Looking back now, he realized she had taken that time to use him for her own benefit.

His mother's death had changed him, he liked to think, for the better.

After that he hadn't been able to trust anyone else. Apart from Andrea. Silvia had been in his face up close and suffocating. He had managed to push her away, but he still ended up enduring her lies through the years. There were some days when he liked the idea that little Alessa might be his, though he knew the chances of that were very slim. But a man could hope.

In her quiet and unassuming way Andrea had been there for him and she hadn't asked for anything in return. With her, he'd had the one relationship where emotional connection, more than the sex, had mattered to him. But he had become too consumed by his mother's death to deal with it. He was still trying to find meaning in his life and Andrea had already found hers. She was a strong, independent woman who was trying to carve out her way in life. They had been good together but had slowly drifted apart.

Out of that was born a firm friendship. They didn't see each other much or talk much. But when either of them needed business advice, they helped each other.

Ava Ramirez had flown straight into his life out of the blue. Alone and very much single, she had appeared at the Casa Adriana on what should have been her honeymoon.

Even though she was beautiful, her mixture of beauty and vulnerability, as well as the circumstances surrounding her, had more than piqued his interest. When she'd mistaken him for a driver, he'd been more than happy to go along with her assumption, even at the risk of looking like a fool to the ever-observant Gina.

They'd had a spark of attraction way back when they had first crashed into each other's lives. One thing had slowly led to another and here he was.

He had started to believe she was falling for him just as surely as he had fallen for her. But just when things were getting better for them both, she had announced her return home.

That a woman would think of leaving him, would pick going back home over him, was not something that Nico Cazale was used to. As pigheaded, and as bigheaded, and as presumptuous as it seemed, this was Nico's world and this situation that he currently found himself embroiled in was one he simply did not know how to handle.

How could he fall for a woman who did not share the same feelings as he did?

He walked over to the window and stared out at the lights illuminating the gardens around the hotel. He felt a strange comfort in the idea of hiding in that darkness. It was easier to deal with life out there than it was in here, where all his failures stared at him so obviously.

He had wanted to celebrate a small milestone—her decision to stay on a little longer—because she had given him hope. Though that wasn't what he'd told her. If he'd told her the truth, he feared she would panic. And so he had played it cool when she had mentioned the possibility of staying on longer to look at clothing.

What had changed?

Andrea and Natale. That's what.

Talk, no matter how small, about past relationships and his history would have done the damage. He knew women talked, and there was no denying that none of it was made up. It was all true. This was what had frightened off Ava.

Ava, who was so sensitive to his past lovers, and his reputation, might have become less enamored after what she heard.

Not for the first time did his reputation precede him. Not for the first time had he come so close to losing her. First over Silvia and Alessa and now this.

Would there always be stories about him? He couldn't control what people said about his past. And he could no more hide his past than he could change it.

In his experience it was all so easy to dump women. But how in the hell was he supposed to make a woman stay?

He clenched his fists and shoved his hands in his pockets. He could not prove himself to Ava now that she had already made her mind up about him. His heart bristled. She was going back to Denver, and she would get busy with her own life. In time she would forget him. And he might try to forget her. He *had* to let her go.

Except that he wasn't about to let Ava Ramirez walk away. Not when it had taken him so many years to find what he believed could possibly be the right woman for him.

One slight problem though, he didn't know, just yet, how he was going to fix this.

Maybe he needed to shift focus for a while, maybe he would focus on his other problem of proving himself to his father.

CHAPTER THIRTEEN

I t had been days since the romantic dinner at the Casa di
Giulietta had crumbled to pieces. Now Ava focused her
mind on the return home.

That night, Nico had driven her back to the pensione and
left without coming in. He hadn't spent a night with her since
and all contact between them had broken down.

Instead of Nico calling her each morning to ask if she
needed a driver, Gina now phoned her instead.

Just like that he wanted nothing more to do with her. She
felt bad for the way in which she had handled the evening. He
had done everything right, had been so romantic and
understanding. His gesture of putting the meal together to
take away her sad memories of the Casa di Giulietta would
have been enough for most women to let bygones be bygones.

Too much champagne had given her the courage and the
audacity to say things she might otherwise have thought twice
about. Now she had gone and messed it all up.

Leaving Nico and returning home were the right things to
do. She had not gone back to the Casa Adriana, nor had she

ventured out to Montova again. Most of her work there was now done. She had talked about returning to Natale's factory for one last time, but that had been when she'd been dragging out her stay here, lengthening her time in Verona, so that she had more time with Nico.

Now she couldn't wait to get away.

But there was one slight problem in her hasty plan. There was still the huge boatload of products to be shipped out. Nico had promised that he would help her. She knew nothing about navigating the muddy waters of freight and international shipments. She needed his help, but she didn't want to ask him for it. But with her return flight now unchanged and in a couple of days' time, she had to be the bigger person and ask for his help.

She had to face him at some time. There was no other way around it. She would go to the Casa Adriana and ask Nico. She would salvage what was left of their friendship. He had always helped her and looked out for her. If he avoided her now, she knew it was because she had hurt him.

She made her way to the hotel. Remembering other such trips in previous days, pangs of sadness gnarled their way around her heart. She could never repay the kindness Nico had shown her and she would feel better about things if they parted as friends. She had started taking this place for granted and now that her time here was almost over, she was feeling the sadness more and more each day.

Ava approached the hotel's reception desk to find Gina rushing around, busy as always, but this morning a little more agitated than she had ever seen her. She prayed that Nico would be in his office.

"Hi, Gina." Ava ventured a glance at the office door, just behind Gina, hoping that Nico would appear. It would be easier for her to speak to him here, with others, than the two of them alone in his office.

Gina looked at her, then turned away. Her usual warm self not much in evidence today. Ava didn't think too much about it, although she found it odd. The thought of facing Nico gnawed away at her.

"Is Nico in?"

"No. He had a meeting in town. He will be back soon." It seemed as if Gina was about to say more but the voice that Ava heard next was Rona's.

Rona?

She dismissed the crazy thought as soon as it appeared, casting doubt on her hearing. Obviously, her anxiety about Nico was getting to her.

"Car-los!"

Ava stepped back and shook her head. It couldn't be.

"Don't just stand there looking at her. Get me a change of clothes, Carlos."

Ava's stomach heaved; she stared in the direction of the conservatory, knowing that *that* voice did not belong *here*.

"Car-los!"

Gina swallowed. "Uh ... I meant to tell you that your family arrived last night—" Before she could finish her sentence Ava charged toward the conservatory. There was no mistaking it.

That was Rona's voice.

It had that edge that could only have come from a highly-strung woman who hadn't slept well in days.

Her sister was here?

The thought filled Ava with dread. A long flight with a young baby couldn't have been easy. Not if she knew her niece. Tori couldn't sit still for more than a couple of minutes.

Carlos being with them would have helped, but Tori would always want her mother over her father, no matter how much Carlos did for her—and he did a lot.

"Ava." A gentle hand on her shoulder from behind startled her. Without even turning around, she knew that touch and instinctively she knew straightaway who it was.

She'd come along, too?

"Mom?" Ava spun around and threw her arms automatically around her mother's small shoulders. The more she held her, the more she realized she needed her mother's hug. "What are you doing here, Mom?" She pulled away, a dozen questions sat on her lips waiting for escape.

"We were worried about you. We wanted to surprise you."

But the words were lost on Ava, whose jaw dropped at the realization that her entire family was now at the Casa Adriana.

Not in Denver. But *here.*

"Worried? Why? I'm flying home in a few days, Mom."

"You are?"

"I am."

Now it was her mother's turn to look shocked. "Well, if I'd have known that, we wouldn't have come out here looking for you."

"I thought I told you."

"No, dear," Elsa said, "You were always very vague about your return date."

Ava's decision to extend her stay even further had fallen through after *that* dinner at the Casa di Giulietta and she hadn't gotten around to changing her return flight anyway. But it didn't matter anymore, because her whole family were now *here.*

She linked arms with her mother, and they walked into the eating area.

Carlos's huge frame was the first thing Ava saw as they stepped into the conservatory. He was busy rummaging through the baby bag and as he pulled out a change of clothes for Tori, his face brightened at seeing Ava.

"Hey, Carlos." She stepped forward and hugged him warmly. Ava got on well with her brother-in-law. Her affinity for him came more from feeling sorry for him having to deal with Rona most of the time. Carlos was also funny and unpretentious, and all round lovable.

"Good to see you, Ava. They were worried about you." He gestured toward Rona, who sat with Tori on her lap near the side of the table. Don't know why; you're looking swell." Tori's face and hands were covered with slime. Rona's eyes met Ava's gaze.

"Ava," she croaked. Rona handed Tori over to Carlos, then got up with a look of trepidation on her face. The two sisters hugged each other stiffly. Rona scrutinized Ava's face, obviously looking for clues. "You look well enough," she concluded. "Do you mind? I'm starving." She fell back into her seat and started eating. Beside her Carlos struggled with an excitable Tori who had made a game out of getting changed. Beads of sweat laced his forehead, and the table setting for him showed a barely touched bowl of soup and bread rolls.

Ava watched her sister stuffing her face. Elsa sat down opposite Rona. It was surreal having her whole family appear out of thin air here in Verona.

Connor coming here had been bad enough. She had just about recovered from his following her to Verona. But the unannounced arrival of her entire family en masse had trumped all as far as shock went.

She expected to wake up anytime soon.

"Tell me again why you were all worried about me?" She tried to word it as politely as she could and directed her question to no one in particular.

"Mom said you met someone. That was enough to give me the heebie jeebies." Rona mopped up her soup with her ciabatta. "Umm-hmm. This is *good!*" She smacked her lips in appreciation.

Ava looked at her mother in disbelief. *Yup, should have left that little morsel of gossip out of the equation. Too late now.*

"Why don't you let Carlos eat now, honey? He's hungry, too," her mother added quietly.

Carlos had finally finished changing little Tori's clothes. "They were *really* worried about you," he confirmed, giving Ava a knowing wink.

"Let me take her, Carlos. You eat." Ava grabbed little Tori from Carlos, scooping her niece up in her arms, and giving her another huge kiss. Tori looked at her dubiously, but as soon as Ava opened her mouth and gushed, "Hey, you!" the little girl knew for sure this was the aunt she had not seen in a while. "I have missed you." Ava peppered the little girl with kisses all over her face.

"I wish they'd told me you were coming back. Had a hard enough time getting my dad to let me have a couple of weeks off." Carlos dug into his food and completely ignored Rona in all of this.

"A couple of weeks?" said Ava in amazement. Tori ran her soft little fingers across her aunt's face. "Did it ever occur to any of you to call and ask me?" She wasn't a teenager anymore that her entire family had to fly around the world looking for her. "Mom?" Ava cried, demanding further explanation.

"Don't get all mad at Mom. Tell us *who* you've met. I thought you came out here to get your life back in order."

Rona had almost licked the plate clean. The waiters discreetly cleared the table.

Ava ignored her sister. "You're staying here for two weeks?" The Casa Adriana wasn't cheap. She wondered how they were going to afford it all.

"I need a break, anyway. I don't see why *you* should have all the fun," Rona replied insolently.

"We don't intend to stay here for more than a few days," her mother said. "We were going to ask you if there were cheaper places that you know about. Where are you staying?"

Carlos muttered something under his breath.

"Ava?" Nico strode in just then, causing Ava's heart to melt. He stood tall and elegant in his dark blue striped suit. Ava watched her sister give him a quick once over before she glared at him, giving him a hard, piercing stare.

Dark, dangerous, tall and sexy, he always stopped hearts wherever he went. She liked that he had the same effect on her sister. But this was not the way she had intended to meet him, not after that awkward night. He held her gaze as he walked over to her, smiling. His movements confused her. He stopped about a foot short of her, which looked odd, especially when he would have normally grasped her waist and kissed her on sight. This time he stood awkwardly, not quite knowing what to do with his hands.

It was a strange moment for her, made more so by the fact that her entire family was witnessing this event and scrutinizing every movement he made.

The eagle-eyed Rona would not miss a thing, and just as Ava started to panic at how things would play out between her and the love interest that had made them all so curious, Nico stepped forward and kissed her lightly on the cheek. "I've been looking everywhere for you," he murmured, loud enough for everyone else to hear, but low enough, with just that hint of seduction in his voice that she knew so well and loved so much.

In a voice she didn't recognize as her own, she said, "My family are here."

"I know. Gina told me." It sounded so silly, the two of them having this stilted, unnatural conversation, both knowing all the while that it was solely for the benefit for her family.

Despite what she thought about him, Nico understood her better than she knew. He turned to her mother, his face all lit up with a smile as he bent down and took her mother's hand and kissed it. "It's a pleasure to meet you, Ms. Ramirez."

Ava was impressed that he had remembered. And she could see that this brief introduction from Nico was all it took for her mother to fall in love with him. Rona, on the other hand, was another matter.

Nico moved toward her. "You must be Rona?" But he didn't venture closer to her. He seemed to understand Rona's don't-you-dare-touch-me look.

"And *you're* the reason my sister extended her stay?" Rona gave him a dangerous smile.

"Actually, no. I don't think you have it quite right. But why don't you ask your sister yourself?" Nico smiled at her good-naturedly and kept his distance. He then shook hands with Carlos quickly and flashed a smile at Tori who was now sitting on Grandma's lap.

"I guess this means I won't be going back in two days' time," moaned Ava, when the silence became unbearable. Glancing at Nico she saw his features visibly relax.

When she got the chance, she would have words with her sister about that fat face of hers.

It had been decided for her. There was no point in returning to Denver. Not now with her family having just arrived on her doorstep. She could use the extra time to ensure that she and Nico parted as friends at least. This charade of theirs only needed to be maintained in front of her family, and Nico had already demonstrated that he was more than ready for the game.

"You're welcome to use the driver to take you around; we have the bigger car, too, if that would help," Nico offered graciously. He was going too far. Was he trying to paint the picture of a saint to her family? He had no right being so nice and helpful to her and her family. It only made her feel even worse.

But Rona had other ideas. "That's a great idea. Why don't you show us around, Ava? You've been here long enough; you must know this place like the back of your hand." She had already started gathering up the bags she had for Tori's clothes and food, while Carlos carried Tori.

Elsa remained seated. "But if you have other plans, we wouldn't want to get in the way."

But you already did, Mom. Ava steeled herself and instead she said, "No, it's fine, Mom. I can show you around." She glared at Nico before adding, "I didn't have any plans for the day anyway."

Nico excused himself and disappeared out of sight, leaving Ava feeling a little empty now that he was gone. She had needed to speak to him, and his sudden departure left her with an annoying sense of unfinished business.

Her mother was saying something to her, but Ava didn't hear her. She had no idea what to do with her family or where to take them. She knew only that she needed to seize this moment to seek out Nico.

"Sorry, Mom. I'll be back. Why don't you all get your things together? I'll see if the driver is ready and then I can show you around Verona."

"Cool dude," Carlos commentated, when Nico had left. "He's a big improvement on Connor, that's for sure."

"He's a charming young man," started Elsa, but Ava was already heading out of the door.

"I'll be back," she said weakly.

CHAPTER FOURTEEN

Ava disappeared into the rest room just off the main lobby. She needed a moment alone to compose herself. It was all getting to be too much.

She snorted at herself, at the thought of a grown woman hiding in the bathroom, hiding from her family and her lover with whom she had just had a spat.

What a fine mess she'd made of everything in her life, and now she didn't know who or what to face first. She didn't have the stomach for more drama.

Added to that, she now had to deal with being around Nico for another couple of weeks.

Along with her family.

And most likely Connor and Silvia, too.

She sat on the toilet seat, clutching her purse, numb. Her heart skipped a beat when the tingle of her cell phone commanded her attention. She quickly retrieved it from her purse and nearly dropped it on the hard floor when she saw Nico's name flash up.

Her hand shook and she was torn between ending the call or letting it ring to voicemail. She didn't want to hear his voice now. Not when she was sitting on a toilet seat, albeit with the seat down. She didn't breathe until it stopped ringing. A few seconds later a voicemail icon appeared. She listened to the message he had left her.

He needed her address so that he could arrange for shipment of her products. Her heart sank with disappointment, but anger buoyed it back up again. What was she expecting from him? Another romantic dinner date?

Furious, she darted out of the toilet and dove straight into Nico's office without knocking on his door. He didn't move a muscle as she stampeded in.

Without uttering a single word, she grabbed a notepad and scribbled down her address.

He watched her, completely unruffled by her performance.

"Here." She flung the notepad at him. "My address. For shipment."

He looked at her with sadness. When her eyes rested on his beautiful face, her anger melted away. "Thank you, for organizing it."

"Are you okay?"

"Yes," she lied.

"Your family seems pleasant enough. I hope they will enjoy their stay here."

Goddamn it. Can't you say how you feel?

"Why the big show—pretending we're a couple?" she asked.

Nico leaned forward at his desk, and in a diplomatic manner, replied, "I didn't want to embarrass you. Isn't that what your family was expecting?"

"You don't have to look out for me, Nico. I'm a grown woman. I can handle the stark truth of the situation."

He acknowledged her request with a nod of his head and

waited for her to continue. But she wasn't falling for his tactic, which was that she would carry on blubbering if he remained quiet. She stood her ground and stared back at him.

"What exactly is the situation?" he asked, still so calm, still so collected. His hands rested easily on the table. He was a man at ease while she stood before him, barely holding back her fury. The calmer he was, the more he riled her.

"I'm going back." She would eventually, when her family left. There was no need to tell him that she would be staying on longer now, just because of them.

"You already told me. You decided for us."

"There is no us."

His face hardened, yet he forced a smile. "As you wish. Could you please shut the door on your way out?" Brown eyes, hardened and glittering with anger, locked onto hers. The electricity in the room cackled. Ava cocked her head slightly, then pulled her broken ego together quickly and lifted her chin high. Nico's gaze dropped from her face to a point on the table. He busied himself with his paperwork and started signing some paperwork. "You just carry on; don't let me keep you."

Ava started to walk off; if she remained here a second longer, she would explode. His cursory dismissal of her frustrated the heck out of her.

Just as she got to the door, Nico said, "I've arranged for the car to be at your disposal. Just let Gina know when you need it."

He was still so good to her. She said nothing and left. It was time to do some sightseeing around Verona.

The Casa di Giulietta was the last place Ava wanted to visit. But her mother, having done her due diligence before she arrived here, asked to see it. So, Ava was obliged to traipse there again.

Memories of her last time here, at that fateful dinner, swept over her, dampening her mood further.

Rona grabbed Ava's arm and slowed her down while Elsa and Carlos ambled around with the stroller, soaking in the atmosphere in the courtyard.

"Tell me some more about this Nico guy."

"You've seen him. He's nice, kind."

"He looks like a playboy and if his daddy owns the hotel, you just hit yourself with the double no-no: a rich playboy."

"I didn't know you could get poor playboys."

The edge was starting to creep into Rona's voice. "I don't understand how you can come here with the so-called intention of clearing your mind—" She used her fingers to illustrate speech marks "— and end up falling for some rich Italian."

"I didn't come looking for him. We just found each other."

"You just found each other. Aaah. *Soooo* romantic." Rona's tone was sarcastic.

"Do you have a problem with him?" Ava shot back.

"My problem is that I don't want you getting hurt again. It's only been a few months since Connor ditched you."

"Can you stop going on about that?"

"I'm looking out for you!"

"I can see that. So much so that you had to fly all the way out here. Did it ever occur to you to call me?"

"Mom said you were staying on for another few weeks."

"Yes, but that was two weeks ago. I was coming home this week." There was no need to tell her sister that she had considered extending her stay for longer.

"Well, we're here now and we might as well make the most of it. It's lovely here. It's all the things you said."

"*You* were the one who told me to be wary of Italian men and that it was a dangerous place for single women."

"Don't say I didn't warn you. I'm here to save you from another failed relationship," Rona retorted.

"I don't need saving."

"Seriously? Are you and this Nico going to lead to anything? A long-distance relationship? Hello?" She cupped her hand to her ear. "Those don't work."

Nico's ploy had worked. Rona giving Ava the third degree about her "impossible" relationship with Nico was not as bad as Rona questioning Ava about what had gone wrong—a conversation she would have been embroiled in had it not been for Nico's intervention.

At least in the eyes of her family, she and Nico were an item. She was thankful to him for having the foresight to think ahead.

The more Rona droned on and on about things she did not like about Nico, and all the things that were wrong with her being with this man, the more Ava got to thinking about their relationship, now that it was dead in the water.

She had pushed all thoughts about them to the back of her mind. Only, having to pretend they were an item meant she was forced to think about it even more. How could it work across two continents? Nico was so busy, and so was she. But it no longer mattered, because she and Nico were no more.

She could put up with the charade of a relationship for a little longer. It would be easier to confess to the breakup once she had returned to Denver.

Rona continued. "Just saying. You might want to think this out carefully before you start making more crazy plans."

"I was here more for business than anything else," Ava cried out.

Rona gave her a leisurely glance. "Yeah, I bet that's what you've been telling yourself."

Ava fumed. What was it with her sister? Had motherhood and the confines of staying at home with the baby turned her all bitter and twisted?

"Do you know what I think, Rona? You don't care about my welfare. You just needed an excuse to get away."

"After your failed wedding, I'm concerned about you. We all are," Rona snapped then stopped and glanced up at the building in front of her. "Is this it?"

"It's the Casa di Giulietta—Juliet's balcony. Mom wanted to see Verona's best loved attraction."

"Right," said Carlos. He stared up at it with a lost expression. "It's just a balcony."

Elsa stepped forward and stared at it, fascinated. "So romantic," she said softly. "I've read about this. And I've rubbed Juliet's breast for good luck, too."

"Mom, you didn't," Ava gasped.

Rona screwed her face up in disgust. "Awww, get a grip, Mom. Since when did you turn into such a romantic?"

But Elsa was lost in her own little reverie. "Come on," she said, giggling with excitement. "Let's go inside and take a proper look."

Ava hesitated, but the expression on her mother's face removed any reservations she might have had about revisiting the room where she and Nico had last dined.

CHAPTER FIFTEEN

"They have an offer which interests me a great deal."

"You said you wouldn't sell out, Papa. You already rejected Luxuriant's offer. Why would you now consider Tambini's?"

Edmondo Cazale sat back in his chair and looked calmly at his son. Nico paced around the room, his face tinged red as his anger got the better of him.

"Calm down, son. You have a lot to learn. Doing a war dance isn't going to prepare you well for meetings with others."

Nico stopped and glared at his father. "I know how to behave in meetings." He forced himself to take a seat in front of his father's desk. "You promised me that you wouldn't be selling out. I told you I can do this. You *know* I'm delivering results. Why are you so set on selling everything you've worked so hard for?"

"Because I am being offered a very good deal. One which is too good to pass up."

Nico rubbed his hands over his face. The cuffs of his shirt were rolled up and wisps of dark hair flecked his bare forearms. Did his father consider him to be such a failure that he wouldn't consider letting him have the reins? "No offer should be good enough, not if you want to leave a legacy."

"A legacy? For whom?"

Nico forced back the growl that threatened to flare up. "It's not even the money, Papa. It's that you spent your life building this, took time away from me and Mama to build this." He threw his arms up, gesturing at the empty space all around him. "And now you say you've had a good enough offer to sell it all to someone? We missed out on a life with you for so many years, just so you can sell out now because you have an offer that's too good to refuse?"

The disgust in his voice was palpable. He continued, unfazed, striking while the iron was hot. "You were never in it for the money. Maybe when I was a boy and Mama lived a sad life without you. We wanted so much for your business to take off. Now you're successful and you have the money, how much more do you need? Isn't it all about leaving something behind?"

The older Cazale slumped back, his shoulders slumping. Yet still he said nothing. Nico sniffed defeat. "We go back and forth, arguing about this the whole time. Why won't you believe me when I tell you that I'm learning? That I'm working hard? That I'm trying to prove myself to you? The hotel capacity is full most of the year round, not just in the peak seasons. We should be expanding, not selling out."

"If I reject Tambini's offer, what then?"

Nico looked at his father steadily, his hands poised just under his chin. "What then? Exactly what we discussed a few weeks ago, Papa. We move forward. We refurbish the other Cazale hotels, and we buy new ones as we see them. We expand, Papa."

He loved his father, and had the utmost respect for him,

but his father tested his patience most of the time. They were two completely different creatures. It had been hard for his mother, he remembered with sadness, trying to be the one beacon of peace between them both.

"Ava's family seems pleasant enough." His father changed the subject completely. "I like her. She seems to be a good influence on you."

Nico shifted in his seat and brought his foot down from his knee. He sat forward. "She is."

That her family had turned up unannounced was not such a bad thing. He wasn't so sure that Ava saw it that way, though. She had been so angry this morning and he wasn't sure that it was all to do with him. In any case, with them here it meant Ava would stay on a while.

Any extra time was a bonus, whether she was talking to him or not. It meant he still had time to make things up with her.

He looked directly into his father's eyes; he wanted to say more, but the words didn't come. Something about a legacy and his plans for a possible future with Ava, but the two ideas evaporated as soon as they started to mesh together in his thoughts.

He turned his attention to business matters instead. "I'm going to look at the Cazale Riccione soon, get it to the same standard as here. There's also a hotel near there that I want to check out." He waited patiently for his father's response and on seeing the hard line of his father's lips, he braced himself.

"I am aware of your ideas about expanding, son, but I am not so sure. It's a big risk. And I'm not one for taking so much risk, not at my age." His father became silent again, weighing up his words carefully. "But I don't see the harm in having a look. Report back to me with your findings."

Nico nodded at his father appreciatively. "I'll do that," he said, trying not to let his excitement show.

CHAPTER SIXTEEN

Sun streamed into the glass conservatory at the Casa Adriana and lifted everyone's spirits.

Verona beckoned for the Ramirez family, and Ava's daily routine had shifted focus dramatically with their appearance.

They had checked out of the Casa Adriana and Nico had arranged for them to stay in the pensione next door to Ava's. They could all have stayed with her but Nico had put them in a separate one and for this she was grateful.

It was hard enough having to spend two weeks with them all here, let alone to share the same living quarters as well. She had a feeling that Nico preferred her to have her own space, too, for reasons of his own.

Maybe he hoped there would be a reconciliation soon. Ava was more determined than ever to let the boundaries stay, now that she had taken the difficult first step of erecting a wall between the two of them. Ever since their last exchange, when she had flung her scribbled note with her address at him, their paths hadn't crossed.

Her family was grateful for Nico's generosity, even Rona who actually admitted to liking Nico for being so generous.

"We could have just shared with you, Ava. I don't like putting your young man to so much trouble," her mother said.

"No, Mom. It's better you all have your own space."

Because I need my own space.

Rona eyed Ava suspiciously. "Yeah, right." A comment Ava chose to ignore completely. But the next words from Rona's mouth had them all entranced.

"Connor?" A blanket of total confusion swept over Rona's face. The same blanket now shared by Connor. "Rona? This is turning into quite a family reunion." A heap of questions lined his face, but he said nothing.

In all the commotion of recent events, Ava hadn't thought to mention news about Connor to her family.

"You're not family," Ava snapped, as she walked past him. "Come on, Mom. Let me show you the gardens. Carlos and Tori are already out there." She grabbed her mother's arm and left, leaving Connor alone with Rona. Being out in the gardens also meant she had less chance of bumping into Nico.

Elsa nodded briefly at Connor, who seemed almost embarrassed to have seen her. Barely a word was exchanged between the two of them.

Rona and Connor glanced at each other warily. Rona surveyed him with the cool gaze of a lioness sizing up her prey. If she was wary around Nico, she hated Connor a hundred times more.

"You're here? What gives?" She circled around the rather bewildered-looking Connor, who stood next to a table, holding onto the back of a chair for dear life.

"I came looking for Ava."

Immediately, her bullshit detector was on full alert. "The

bride you ditched?" She didn't try to hide the toxicity in her sarcasm.

Connor seemed to utter something, but the words disappeared before they reached her ears. She jabbed a finger at him.

"What makes you think my sister's crazy enough to have any feelings left for you?"

"The same thing that brought you out here, after her." Connor was cool and composed, almost back in his lawyer role. "She's confused, mixed up and she's not sure what she wants."

Rona readied herself to expel a string of choice words with the sole intent of reducing him to a quivering wreck but a tall, gazelle-like blonde trotted in, with an enormous pair of sunglasses resting on top of her hair.

"Connor!" The words sang out of her mouth.

"Silvia."

Dark, pouty lips air kissed each side of Connor's cheeks. Rona looked on, dumbstruck, as the woman ran a perfectly manicured fingernail gently across his face. It was only then that the woman appeared to notice her for the first time.

Pouty lips voiced, "And you are?"

Rona had forgotten to breathe, and now she choked on her own breath. She gave Connor the filthiest look and ignored the woman completely. "And you came out looking for who?" She stormed out.

No matter that she and Ava didn't see eye to eye, Rona really did mean to look out for her younger sister. She was so consumed by anger at the sheer gall of Connor not only being here but also flaunting his latest floozy with him, that she walked headfirst into Nico.

One look at his tall and toned body in his charcoal gray suit and his sharply chiseled features had Rona doing a double take. Her pulse quickened at her annoyance. She didn't like her reaction to Ava's man, this no-good, playboy Italian. He would only go and break her sister's heart all over again.

But damnit, he was to die for. Could she really blame Ava for tripping over her high heels and falling for someone like him?

"Good morning, Rona."

She had to give it to him: the man was polite, if nothing else. But she had him figured out, that slimy, slick air he put on. He might be good looking, but she could see past him.

She was tempted to give him a cutting reply, take him down a peg or two, but she quickly remembered that this man had put them up in a pensione and he had been more than gracious to her family. She gave a rudimentary shake of her head as they both found themselves standing opposite each other, caught in an uncomfortable deadlock, with nothing much to say.

Nico smiled and she did not. "Nice place you have here." She went for the polite angle.

"Thank you."

"Please don't go giving my sister any crazy idea about romance." She cut quickly to the chase. There was no point wasting time on frivolous small talk.

She watched Nico's jaw tighten, thrilled that she had one-upped him.

He glared back; she had ruffled his feathers all right. He clearly didn't want her meddling around in his business, telling him what to do with his love life. But heck, Ava was her sister, and she was only looking out for her. These well-oiled, moneyed smarty pants was not going to get into her sister's panties—or stay there too long, now that he was probably in them. Not if she could help it.

Besides, she hadn't such a great night with Tori not

sleeping properly ever since they'd arrived. Rona was looking for someone to take her anger out on. Nico looked a worthy shot.

But as they eyed each other across the checked and marbled lobby floor, Silvia and Connor walked right past them.

Silvia jabbered away, and Connor seemed captivated by each word she uttered. Nico raised an eyebrow, and without knowing the reason why, Rona could tell he was more than a little pissed off himself at the sight of them.

Why was he so bothered by them?

"This gets more surreal with each passing day," Rona muttered to herself.

***

"They're an interesting family."

The ever calm and serene Gina beamed at Nico over her computer screen. From her vantage point at the reception desk, hidden behind the screen, she had a great window for witnessing the hellos, goodbyes and other dramas that were played out daily in this lobby.

She knew almost everything that was said and done here. And in that respect, she was all-knowing.

Nico walked toward her, looking more frazzled than she had seen him in a long time. She had a feeling that romance and relationships, two 'R's that Nico had readily avoided up until now, were starting to take their toll on him.

She waited until he was at her side. "At least Ava will be around a little longer. That's got to be a good thing?" She wanted him to open up to her, because lately, from what she could tell, he had nobody else to turn to. He shrugged his shoulders helplessly.

He played it cool and smooth, as if he didn't care, when his face said otherwise. Things always went according to Nico Cazale's plans.

Except now he had the Ramirez family, his ex-girlfriend, and his new girlfriend's ex-fiancé all within close range.

This was better than daytime TV.

CHAPTER SEVENTEEN

Silvia sounded like a fast-forwarded recording when she was in full flow.

She strode around the hotel car park, screeching rapid-fire Italian into her cell phone. Connor hovered around her silver Mercedes Benz convertible, blowing imaginary dust off the sleek leather headrest. For a man who was used to only thinking about himself, Ava found it a complete 180-degree turn to find him now keeping watch on Silvia's car while pretending to be invisible so that she could talk on the phone.

He had never been like that around *her*.

Engrossed as he was by the cleanliness of the convertible, he didn't notice Ava walking toward him. Catching Connor almost alone without Silvia's handcuffs was a rare event these days. Ava welcomed the chance to have a quiet word with him, while Elsa waited inside. Being outside also meant she would be away from Nico, who was probably in his office. It didn't help that every waking moment of her day was filled with thoughts of him. She was lost and in limbo and she could not even go home.

Instead, she was forced to endure the thought that she might see him and they'd end up having another cold exchange. She didn't want that.

"Hey." Talking to Connor was much easier than facing Nico. Also, the fact that he now seemed to be involved with Silvia, made it more comfortable for her to approach him.

"Hey." He slid his hand across the car door and examined the dust on his fingers.

"I see you've found a new reason for staying here." There was a playfulness in Ava's voice as she glanced over at Silvia.

"Who knows?" He jerked his head in Silvia's direction. She was too wrapped up in her conversation to notice he had company.

Ava leaned against the car door and smiled at Connor. "It seems so surreal to see you here and now my family, too."

"They were always so protective of you."

Ava blanched. "Were they?"

"Always." His resoluteness made her wonder if he had always felt this way about them. She knew her family could have that effect on some people; she had never considered that Connor had been bothered by it. It didn't matter anymore.

"What's the deal with Silvia? Did you come out here looking for love?"

"Did you?" He gave her a pained look. Was Connor really upset by the idea of her and Nico being together? He didn't know that she and Nico had had an argument and she wanted to keep it that way.

"I came here to find peace and to heal. It was never my intention to find love." She was being more honest than she had bargained on.

"It was my intention. I came looking for you."

"You must have looked for all of two hours, max."

"I came here wanting to get you back."

No, not that again.

"Come back to me, Ava."

She shook her head. It was too much too soon, she was still dealing with the maelstrom of emotions because of her break from Nico. Connor was nowhere near her radar. She hadn't bargained on their conversation getting so heavy.

"We can make it work, Ava. Give me the chance to make it up to you." Connor seemed to be speaking from the heart. Gone was the rough, arrogant face mask he wore most of the time. He was stripped bare to the soul and his eyes carried an expression of something akin to regret. She felt he meant every word he said.

Why now? Why here? Why at all?

Was every waking minute of her time from here onwards to be filled with complications? Ava straightened up and pushed her hands into the back pockets of her jeans. She shook her head, staring at the steps in front of her. "Why?"

"Because I love you. It took losing you to find out what I had. I'm an idiot."

She jerked her head up at him, meeting his scrutinizing gaze head on. This really was too much for him to throw at her now. "You're wasting your time."

"I won't give up. I came to Venice for you, I'm here in Verona for you."

Ava let out a laugh, almost as if a strawberry had caught in her throat and she was trying to cough it out. "*That* was your attempt at getting me back?" She thought back to the uncomfortable moment when he had walked in on her and Nico, in Venice.

"I didn't expect you to jump into bed with the first person you saw."

"He was not the first person—" Ava started to remonstrate, her face growing hotter by the second.

Except he was. Nico had been the very first person she had come across the minute she had landed in Verona. She blushed. What must it have looked like to everyone else? "I don't know why you came all the way out here, after what you did. Why? You're crazy to think I'd go back to you. I mean, was that your lousy attempt to win me back; a day in Venice and then you come here and find someone else? That tells me all I need to know. You're not the type of man who settles down, Connor."

He seemed suddenly preoccupied with the dust on the car door and ran his fingers against the top of the window. "I mean it, Ava. I want you back. You're having a little holiday fun. It's understandable. I hurt you and now you want to play the field a little."

Holiday fun? She stepped away from the car, hands akimbo. "It's not holiday fun. It's more than that. More than I ever had with you." The moment she said these words, they rang true for her.

Nico was more than Connor had ever been, even in the short amount of time she had known him. He had shown her more consideration and cared more for her than Connor ever had in the whole time they had been together.

It was too big a revelation to dwell on. She quickly pushed this thought away, resolving to think about it later.

"When you're over him, I'll still be waiting for you, Ava. Remember that. If not here, then back home."

"You've met your match, Connor."

As if on cue, Silvia looked up. She quickly ended her conversation and slunk across to Connor.

"Ready, darling?" She flashed him a blinding smile, half acknowledging Ava before climbing into her car. She didn't even wait for Connor. The poor man had to quickly jump in and the car soon sped away.

"Nice talking to you, too," muttered Ava, under her breath, as the car disappeared out of view.

For the first time she was relieved that Silvia had come to her rescue.

CHAPTER EIGHTEEN

The next few days saw the family settle into the pensione and see more of Verona.

Nico had provided a driver for them to use at their leisure, the thoughtfulness of which elevated him further in Elsa's eyes.

Rona, though, had told Ava that as far as she was concerned, if her sister was sleeping with the son of the hotel owner, surely some privileges were due.

Ava could see that this 'vacation' was far from the relaxing time her sister had envisaged. Traveling with a young child made that impossible. The family had only been around the town center in Verona and seen a few of the popular sights.

Most days they managed a stroll around Verona, where Rona could window shop. It was a good enough compromise. Carlos tagged along, eager to try the different restaurants if only to pick fault with them. Nothing was as good as the restaurants his family owned.

With her family keeping her occupied, Ava managed to avoid Nico easily. Distance apart gave her time to ruminate on matters, but as a result she ended up wanting to be with him, rather than not.

Taking time out with her mother was the best tonic. She was therefore thankful that Rona was busy with her baby and Carlos.

On this March morning, Ava wanted to take her mother out further, not just to the town center where she had been more than content to while away her days.

There had been no need to go to Montova these days, and her last meeting with Andrea had left a bad feeling with Ava. She avoided getting back in touch with her even though she needed to conclude her shipment details. For the time being, all matters relating to her online store were relegated to the back of her mind.

Today, for some reason, she felt the urge to return to Montagnano, to the place where Nico had grown up. It held a special place in her heart because it was off the beaten path, calm and comforting. She reassured herself it was nothing to do with memories of the last time Nico had taken her there.

Her mother was eager to visit a new place and Ava was happy to have the luxury of spending another day with just the two of them.

"Didn't you ask your sister to come with us?" Elsa asked gently.

Ava shook her head. "No, Mom. I wanted it just to be the two of us today." The finality in her voice stopped any further questions her mother might have had.

Ava had avoided Rona ever since they had spoken about Nico. No one in her family asked why she and Nico didn't spend much time together. So far, nobody suspected that things between them had cooled. She didn't want to risk the truth leaking out by letting Rona pry deeper.

Elsa let out a low sigh. "I wish the two of you would get on."

Ava slid her arm through her mother's as they made their way toward the cozy little parade of shops at the start of the village.

"It looks like a picture postcard. So pretty. I like this place already." Elsa looked around approvingly.

Ava held her mother's arm close by her side. "It's nice to have you here, Mom." The last time she had come here was with Nico. Was this the time she had realized he was turning out to be more than a friend?

"Tell me some more about Nico," her mother said.

"I didn't come here looking for him, Mom."

"I know."

"I came here to clear my head."

"I know."

"I bumped into him the first day, as soon as I landed. I thought he was a driver from the hotel." Ava let out a little laugh, remembering her confusion at the beginning of her vacation.

They carried on walking along the small, cobbled streets, past the row of shops and restaurants until they came to a small stream—the same place where she and Nico had had their first kiss. She sat at the same bench where they had sat. Ava felt her eyes prick with tears—of sadness or joy, she wasn't sure which. The day was beautiful, idyllic. She loved being here with her mom. So why did she suddenly feel the need to be with Nico again?

She looked away and stared at the sky, hoping the wetness in her eyes would disappear. Trying to appear busy, she looked through her bag and pulled out the velvet box.

"I want to show you something," she said to her mother. She opened the box to reveal the breathtaking

Flamentagostini bracelet. She had worn it when she was with Nico, feeling safer wearing such an expensive item with him around. But ever since that dinner at Juliet's balcony, she had stored it back in the box.

Elsa gasped. "It's beautiful!"

"Try it on," Ava encouraged.

Elsa shook her head. But Ava pulled the bracelet out carefully and handed it ot her mother who inspected it carefully, examining the dazzling jewels and beads amid the delicate metalwork.

"Nico bought this for me after I saw it in a jeweler's shop here."

"He must care for you a great deal." Elsa handed the bracelet back.

"He does," said Ava in a faraway voice.

"I was worried about you."

"No guessing who put that idea in your head."

A group of elderly women shuffled past, laughing, the wrinkles on their faces showing signs of a life well lived.

I could easily grow old here. The thought flashed quickly through Ava's mind.

Elsa remained silent. "Rona loves you. She's always looked out for you, Ava. We don't want you to get hurt anymore." She patted her daughter's knee.

They gazed at the water in front of them, for it was difficult to look anywhere else. The peaceful trickle of the gently running water and the way it slowly flowed was a calming experience. It had been so peaceful and serene that it had completely made her and Nico feel at ease, dropping their inhibitions and revealing their true feelings for one another.

"I'm not hurting, Mom," she lied. "The future has never

looked so good. I've got lots of ideas for my website." But her voice was flat.

"Is there any reason for you to stay here for much longer?" Elsa seemed determined to take her daughter home with her. Luckily for her, Ava had the same idea.

"No reason at all. I'm flying back with you all. When are you going back?"

"Next week."

Ava nodded. One more week she could handle. Maybe she needed to check with Nico and make sure he had the shipment side of things locked down.

"It's lunchtime. Let me take you to a wonderful little place where you can try the most delicious panino."

"Panino?" Her mother echoed. Ava nodded and got up, offering her mother a hand to grab as she got up. "And afterwards, I'll take you to a gorgeous little jeweler's shop, if it's open."

CHAPTER NINETEEN

With its fountains, waterfall and picnic tables, the Parco delle Cascate di Molina was a delightful place to spend the day.

Carlos half ran, half walked, carrying his precocious little Tori in his arms; the little girl squealed with delight as he swung her around like an aeroplane.

Ava sat on the park bench with her mom and sister. But her thoughts were occupied by Nico, as they had been ever since her return from Montagnano yesterday. Her family still had not cottoned on to the fact that she and Nico weren't exactly on speaking terms. The more time they spent apart, the more she felt the pull to see him.

Rona got up, tottering precariously on her high wedges. There were no signs of baby weight gain in her tight jeans and tight-fitting V-necked top. Her huge golden hoop earrings shouted, "Look at me" and her bright makeup lit her up like a neon sign in the dark of night.

"Not so high, Carlos!" she yelled. "She's just had milk."

Carlos jerked his head up and nodded before scooting Tori around on his arms. He had not shaved in days and looked like death, but he was smiling, having the time of his life.

Ava and her sister had come to some sort of truce since their early falling out over Nico and their ideas on Italian men.

"I'm so glad Gina told me about this place. I knew Tori would love it here," Ava enthused.

"Carlos, too," added Elsa, watching her son-in-law. "At least he seems happier today."

Rona dropped her news. "He's smiling for a reason."

"And what's that?" Ava asked.

"He's going back early, says his dad can't get the staff and it's a busy time. They're short staffed as it is."

"Going back early?" Ava asked. "We're all going back next week. What's the rush?"

Rona chewed gum loudly. "Carlos says he's tired of sightseeing."

"I'm sure that's not all he's tired of," Ava muttered.

"Are you going to tell her, or shall I?" Rona glanced at her mother.

Ava turned her head slowly. She looked at her mother's side profile, but her Elsa refused to meet her stare. "Tell me what, Mom?"

"Oh, just that—" Elsa cleared her throat a little nervously, "we've extended our stay."

"You did what?" Ava almost shouted. She looked from Rona's bright cherry lips to her mom's creased face. Her mother smiled and the creases deepened around her mouth.

"We thought we'd stay here a little longer, now that we've come all this way."

Ava's heart thumped wildly. No. God, no. What were they thinking? She didn't want this. Didn't need it. She needed to go back home. She needed to be away from Nico.

"Mom." Ava stared at her mother, her eyes ablaze with anger.

"Look at the plus side: you get to spend more time with your lover boy." Rona threw her a contemptuous look. "Or is he not your lover boy anymore? Come to think of it, how come you two hardly spend any time together?"

Ava's defenses shot right back up again. Ignoring Rona's threatened assumption of the situation, she barked, "And where do you think you're going to stay?"

If they stayed on, it meant she would need to speak to Nico about having the pensione longer. She would need to ask him for things and the thought of it made her uneasy. She was always asking him for things, or he was always willing to help her. He was there for her, whether she wanted him to be or not. She blushed at the thought of how needy she must seem.

"We'll find another pensione if the one we are in is no longer available. Sorry, honey. The last thing I'd want is to put your friend out. I don't want to make you feel ashamed about us."

Ava hastily jumped in. "No, Mom. Don't be silly. Me ... Nico...," she stumbled, looking for the right choice of words.

Her mother's gentle voice interrupted her thoughts. "What is it?"

"I'm sure the pensione is fine. I'll check with Nico. How much longer are you planning on staying?" She didn't dare look at Rona. For all her hesitations and reservations about Italy and Ava coming here, Rona seemed to be enjoying her holiday far more than she was letting on.

But problems would arise soon enough with Carlos leaving. Rona would have to look after Tori herself. Ava smiled at the idea of her sister having to do double duty with her husband gone.

Then another thought occupied her mind: Rona was so selfish and self-obsessed; she would think nothing of making her poor mother stand in for Carlos. Anything to make Rona's life a little easier.

Just then Carlos staggered toward them, carrying Tori in his arms. The little girl's cheeks were flushed red, and she looked beyond exhausted. They all bunched together on the bench to make room for Carlos's large frame.

"She'll sleep well tonight." Rona took out a bottle of water and gave it to her daughter.

"I'll sleep even better," Carlos said, wiping the sweat off his brow. "Got anything to drink?" he asked his wife and when Rona shook her head he grunted and took the bottle from Tori. He drained it dry.

"What did you do that for?" Rona's hooped earrings dangled dangerously. Carlos wiped his wet lips with the back of his hand and gave her a smile.

Elsa got up prematurely. "Let's get some lunch. I saw a lovely little place on the way here."

Ava wasn't done yet. She nudged Carlos gently in the side. "I hear you're going back early."

"I must. The restaurant's real busy now. If we'd have planned this better, I mighta been able to get time off, but this trip was rushed. My dad's struggling. I need to get back."

Ava got up slowly. "How much longer are you staying?" she asked again, directing her question to no one in particular.

"They should stay as long as they want," Carlos said eagerly, his face all lit up with glee.

Ava couldn't help but sympathize with the man. Any time away from Rona would be a blessing for him. He worked hard at the restaurant, often until the early hours of the mornings and alternate weekends, too, and still did the most of the looking after for Tori when he was at home. It was obvious enough to see. The poor man needed a break.

"Another couple of weeks." Her mother slipped her arm through Ava's as the rest of their party walked on ahead.

"Something wrong? I thought you might like the idea of staying a bit longer. I'm assuming, of course, that you'll go back when we do. I just thought we might as well make the most of our visit now that we're here. Two weeks seems a short amount of time. I've been reading through the guidebooks and there are so many interesting places to visit. Your father would have loved it here."

These words touched a nerve in Ava and she hugged her mother's arm closer to her. Her mother still missed their father, even after all these years. Ava missed him, too, though her memories of him were hazy and out of focus. She had only been eight and Rona nine when he'd gone out to pay some bills and had never come back home again. Another car had jumped the red light and crashed into her father's, killing him instantly.

Hearing her mom say she missed him now made Ava feel sad, more so at the realization that her mother's life had been a lonely one, and that neither she nor her sister had stopped to think about it. She carried on walking and patted her mom's arm, suddenly overcome with emotion and unable to speak.

She stopped as an idea came to her. It would help get her mom out of the child-minding duties that she felt sure would be heading her way once Carlos had gone.

"Is he always so busy? Nico? It's just that I haven't seen the two of you together much."

"He's busy," Ava replied.

Rona and Carlos had rushed off ahead and she was thankful there were no prying ears around. She wondered whether she would be able to fix things with Nico. Perhaps not get back into the relationship side of things, not that she would fight anything if it happened, but at least to remain friends. He had been there for her at a time in her life when she had needed someone.

Ahead in the distance, Rona had stopped outside a restaurant.

It was Gioberti's. Ava had been there before, and the owner was a flirt. She instinctively knew that Rona would love this place. As she saw her sister's hips swaying from side to side with more exaggeration than usual, butt out, chest out, and her gold hoops swinging wildly, Ava knew they would end up eating there.

"That's the restaurant I had my eye on," Elsa mused.

This should be interesting, Ava thought, watching Gioberti slide away from other patrons and head toward the table where Rona was maneuvering the stroller.

She saw the oh-so-smooth run of Rona's hand through her hair, the disarming giggle, the slight turn of the head as Gioberti pulled out a chair for her while Carlos helped Tori into her highchair.

Ava looked on with amusement. "And she told *me* to be wary of Italian men!"

CHAPTER TWENTY

Nico sat in his car and braced himself for another day.

It had been a week since the dinner at Juliet's balcony, but already it felt like a month. Now that he was back to sleeping alone, he found he couldn't fall asleep easily. He missed the way Ava's warm body curled up against his. Now he spent most of the night restless and woke up drained.

Every waking moment she appeared in his thoughts. Their time in Venice replayed over and over in his mind. A word, a snippet of conversation, something she said—all these things and more would creep back to remind him of her. He missed her. But there wasn't much he could do about it. Especially now that her family was here.

He scraped his hand over his face and took a deep breath. In time, this would all fade away. She would return and he would forget. But for now, he had to get through each day knowing there was a chance he might see her. He hoped for this daily. It was a constant guessing game.

He got out of his car and rushed up the steps. As he walked through the doors, a familiar laugh from the sofa corner immediately put his hairs on edge. He didn't have to turn, for he knew that sound distinctly. But he turned anyway and saw Silvia sitting on one of the sofas, one leg crossed low over the other. She threw her head back and laughed. Connor sat beside her like a besotted puppy. He whispered into her ear and she laughed again.

Nico turned away and headed for his office but his face froze as he headed in that direction.

Was that *Ava* talking to his *father?* His eyebrows scrunched together as he came to a stop just as he reached the reception desk.

Gina was still busy with a group of women who looked ready to leave. And sure enough, beside her stood Ava deep in conversation with his father.

What could they be talking about? What was more, his father was smiling. He even, God forbid, looked happy.

Feeling left out, Nico eased his shoulder blades back, releasing the tension in his neck and shoulders. Ava had her back to him, and his father was so entranced by her that he barely noticed Nico's presence.

From where he stood, observing but not yet noticed by the object of his interest, Nico's eyes ran over each detail of Ava, taking in her long, lean body, her high ponytail revealing her long neck, a neck he very much wanted to run his lips over. His heart beat a little faster and the tension in his lower body went up a notch.

Just at that very moment she turned around and laughed as she stepped back from his father. His father laughed, too, and the very idea of such a relaxed and easy camaraderie between these two made him happy and jealous all at once. He felt the odd one out, as if he could not interrupt their little talk.

"Hi," said Ava. She blushed at the sudden unexpected sight of him. The giveaway color of her cheeks boosted his confidence. Her eyes met his and they locked gazes, each of them trying to work out where the other was at.

"Hello," returned Nico, pleasantly enough. He walked around the side to where they were and nodded at his father, who sobered up when his son approached.

Just as he found the words to say something, Ava turned back to his father and completely ignored him.

"Thank you so much, Mr. Cazale. I'll suggest it to my mom. I'm sure she would like it, if you don't mind."

"Please do, Ava. I could do with some time out. It would be my pleasure."

What would be his pleasure?

Ava gave Edmondo a heartwarming smile and Nico waited for her to look his way. She looked so casual and yet sexy in her white shirt and skinny jeans that he wanted to grab her and rush her back to her pensione.

"See you around." That was all she said to him. Even her smile was halfhearted, and she lowered her eyes, not quite meeting his gaze as she left.

Nico felt cheated. He stared after her, his heart slamming against his ribs as she disappeared out of sight.

That's it? He wanted to run after her. To make up. To sort out their current lack of communication. But his pride stopped him.

"What was that all about?" Nico asked, forcing a touch of nonchalance into his voice. He wouldn't put it past his father to notice that things had cooled a little between them.

The obvious giveaway being the fact that he was now sleeping back at the family home.

"It seems they have extended their stay here." His father pushed his glasses back up the bridge of his nose.

Had he heard right? "Really?" He felt a mixture of excitement and anger well up inside him. Excitement leading to hope for the possibilities that this might bring to him and anger that Ava had not decided to tell him herself.

"Her mother likes it here and wants to spend a little more time. You'll have to see to it that their time at the pensione is extended."

More anger flamed up. "Is that what she came to talk to you about? Extending the stay at the pensione?"

Edmondo shook his head slowly, his mind preoccupied by some paperwork that Gina had handed him.

"She wanted to ask me about a few places to visit around Verona."

And she asked you?

Nico moved his shoulders up and down, hoping to ease the tension that was now building up into the mother of all headaches.

The fact that Ava had gone to the trouble of asking his father, when she could just as easily have asked him, told him how much she hated having anything to do with him.

He bristled with resentment.

Edmondo elaborated further. "Her mother would like to go sightseeing and Ava asked me for recommendations."

"And?" This was adding fuel to the fire; Ava was deliberately avoiding him. "How much longer are they staying?"

"I don't know. Didn't she mention anything to you?"

CHAPTER TWENTY-ONE

"And have a nice time, too." Ava watched her suddenly shy mom walk out of the door with the silver-haired, older Cazale.

Mission accomplished.

She was proud of herself. She had managed to get the two of them out before Rona had returned from the airport after seeing Carlos off.

No Carlos meant no babysitter. And Ava wanted to make sure her mom got the holiday that she deserved.

With yet another extension to her time here, Ava was considering the idea of taking a trip back to Venice or visiting Siena even. Siena might be better, she thought. Venice held too many memories of Nico.

Anywhere would do. She just needed to get away for a few days, to put distance between herself and the man who haunted her. Try as she would, she couldn't stop thinking about him. If it wasn't for her family keeping her occupied, her resolve would have weakened days ago.

The fleeting glimpse she had had of him yesterday when she was talking to Mr. Cazale had gotten her heart racing again. That man caused her body to physically react. And for the rest of the day and last night she had been unable to stop thinking about him.

She could ask her mother to come along, too.

Neither she, nor Rona, had ever considered that their mother might be lonely or that having a companion in her life might be the thing she needed. Selfishly, they had not really considered that their mother might have ideas about seeing anyone.

But the more Ava stopped to think things through, the more she realized there was no reason why her mother could not. She had a great social life back home and kept herself busy with her various book clubs and with helping at the local shelter. She'd also started taking art classes with her neighbor, but mostly, her mother's circle comprised of women: single, divorced or widowed women who were all similar in age to Elsa.

Yesterday when Ava had dropped by the Casa Adriana to pick up some leaflets about places to visit in and around Verona, and to ask Gina, she had wondered if she might also bump into Nico. It was only because Mr. Cazale had happened to walk past that he overheard her asking about local places to visit and he had offered her some advice. He also told her that he would be more than willing to show her mother the sights. His kind suggestion had at first surprised Ava, and she was ready to dismiss it, believing him to be acting out of politeness. But the more she thought about it, the more she realized that it was not such a bad idea after all.

Mr. Cazale appeared to be genuinely excited to show off his hometown. Relaying this news to her mother had been a little harder. "But I hardly know him," Elsa had protested.

"Mom, you saw him every morning at breakfast when you stayed at the hotel."

It was true, Edmondo Cazale had been the very epitome of graciousness on the few occasions that he had met her family. But understandably, her mother still seemed a little uneasy about the idea of spending a whole day with him.

He was, after all, rather distinguished and good-looking.

He was also a widower. And her mother was a widow; she didn't think it seemed right. Ava felt there was nothing wrong with it. They were only going sightseeing together.

Her mother's protestations aside, here they were, both going off for the day to visit the Duomo. Ava knew her mother would love it.

She watched as the chivalrous Mr. Cazale opened the passenger side door for her mother, who, she could see even at this distance, blushed with embarrassment. Ava giggled to herself and turned away. Time to get down to business. There was a small matter she had to take care of.

She turned around, expecting to see Gina at the reception desk but instead she found herself staring right into Nico's glittering dark eyes. They had both avoided each other up until yesterday, and then last night she had tossed and turned in bed, dreaming of those eyes. She couldn't look at him without showing how she felt—she was mad about him. But she knew that she couldn't get involved with him, because to do so meant more heartache.

And yet, aside from the rumors and the gossip, all his actions where she was concerned, had been for her own good.

But she still could not bring herself to trust him. Not after Connor.

Or could she?

Was it too much to hope that he could change?

"We meet again." Dark eyes fixed on her face, and she felt the familiar magnetic pull toward him. Protecting herself, she stepped back and felt the cold glass doors hard against her back.

"Hello, Nico." She managed a smile, hoping that he could not read her desire to kiss those beautiful lips of his.

She dragged her gaze away from the curve of his mouth and struggled to keep a cool composure. But looking into his eyes, standing so close to him, she could feel the heat from his body. Rational thoughts tossed right out of her head.

She had come to read his moods and she knew he wanted to talk things over.

He took a step toward her and pointed outside; surprise strewn across his face. "Is that my father with your mother?"

"It is. Your father kindly agreed to show my mother around."

"Interesting."

"What's so interesting?" she asked, struggling to push her body further back but found herself hemmed in between the doors behind her and Nico in front.

"To see my father taking some time out, for a change."

Ava gazed at his eyes, trying to find the meaning in them, to see if he was being sarcastic or not. But he genuinely seemed pleased.

"Carlos has gone back. Rona's at the airport seeing him off. I thought it would be good for my mom to see a bit of this city, without my niece or my sister in tow." She felt she needed to give him an explanation, but her superfluous words only made him arch an eyebrow at her.

He crossed his arms over his chest, and the clear outline of strong shoulders and biceps only made her heart rate quicken. An image of their naked, slick bodies grinding together accosted her thoughts.

As if he could read her mind, Nico let out a subtle smile, his gaze penetrating her soul. He was so close now that if he stared at her like that a moment longer, she would surrender. Her body yearned for his touch, even though her head knew better.

Disturbing the charged moment between them, he said, "How perceptive of you."

"Oh?" she asked, disappointed that he could still carry on talking when their bodies had other ideas.

"I've seen your little niece, a bundle of energy, very charming. I watched her father dote on her, the lucky man."

"Oh."

He said something, but Ava had stopped listening to his words, and her gaze fell once again to his lips as he carried on talking. Naked images refused to leave her head.

"Yes."

"Yes?" Nico cocked his head at her questioningly. "Yes, what?"

Whatever you say.

"Ava?" He was so close now that she only had to tip her head forward and their lips would touch.

Get a grip.

Say something.

"I think ... your father will be great company."

Nico stared at her lips for the longest time, and without realizing it, she licked hers in anticipation. He tipped his head an inch and the scent of his cologne ratcheted up the color and vibrancy of her mental images. She breathed again, caught up in his aura of sexiness. Everything about him, his lips, his eyes, just *him* only millimeters away from her, sent her heart rate off the Richter scale. Ava half-closed her eyes and parted her lips, waiting for the feel of his soft, wet mouth.

"I'm sure you're right," he whispered. And then he pulled away. By the time her eyelids flew open he had already taken two long strides away from her.

She wanted to scream. But she held it in.

With lips pursed together, she started forward and willed her legs to walk up to the reception desk. Nico stood behind it. She stayed where she was, needing the safety of the high wooden ledge between them. Beneath her ribs, her heart still thundered uncontrollably.

Where was Gina?

It was safer to talk to him with a third person around. She examined his face for clues that he had experienced anything, even a little of what she just had. But it was the picture of perfect calm. As though he hadn't just taken her from zero to sixty in a couple of seconds and shunted her to earth with a thump.

She took a guidebook from the pile on the side, needing to have something in her hands, some sort of armor, no matter how flimsy.

She cleared her throat. "My mom and sister have extended their trip by a few weeks. Would it be all right for them to continue staying at the pensione, if it's not already booked out? If it is still available ..." She heard her voice falter and hated herself for sounding so weak. It was hard asking him for yet another thing. Harder now that they had fallen out.

And after what had *almost* just happened minutes ago, more so.

Before she twittered on, Nico cut her short. "It's not a problem. Of course they can stay. Both pensiones are available. It's still a quiet time here in Verona."

He took the now rolled up travel guide from her hands and the slightest brush of his fingers on hers made her jump. "We seem to have reached some sort of impasse." He waited for her response.

But she was unable to speak. Her face burned. She knew

they needed to sort things out. She just wasn't prepared for it to be right now. Not while she was still recovering from the effect he had on her. Her insides clenched tightly. Before she could say another word, the words fell out of Nico's mouth faster than she could react.

"I'm sorry, Ava."

She had been expecting to argue with him, but his words took her completely by surprise. Dark eyes twinkled at her as his gaze held her captive, before dipping lower to her lips. Strong hands reached out for hers.

No, not again. She could not allow him to do this to her again, just minutes after the last time.

"I know that gossip and rumors hurt and what you hear about me has a basis in reality because I was a player. But I'm a changed man now. I left that life behind years ago. Maybe I'll still pay the price each time my past hits me in the face. But the last thing I want is for you to get hurt. I've missed you, Ava. Can we at least be friends, if nothing else?"

She had been expecting a long, drawn-out attack, more bickering, and then a delicious round of making up. Only he had gone and apologized straightaway, taking out all the intermediate steps.

Only the last one remained.

"Okay." She was not about to tell him that she had missed him, too, or that she was thankful for a few more weeks in Verona.

"Friends?" asked Nico, pulling her hand gently until she was forced to lean in toward him, the wooden ledge between them preventing their bodies from touching. "Ava?" He shot her one of his smoldering, heart-melting looks, and all thoughts about discussing his past love life vanished from her mind.

She had been given more weeks with him. It made sense to make the most of them, and that meant no bickering at all.

"Friends," she said, a little stiffly, but the stiffness melted the moment he brought his lips down to hers.

She was touched by electricity that surged through her. Any attempt at playing it cool disintegrated as soon as his tongue sought out hers. She gave in to his urgency and kissed him back with a fervor that took her by surprise.

"That looks painful," Silvia purred.

Beside her Connor echoed, "Get a room for chrissake."

Ava and Nico pulled apart and she found herself with Connor and Silvia on either side of her. By the time Ava had registered their presence, Gina reappeared from the side door.

"Good morning to you all!" Gina trilled. She slid her petite frame behind the reception desk and beamed at them as if it was a normal occurrence to have such a coterie gathered around the desk, none of whom were checking in or out.

"Breakfast?" asked Connor, turning to Silvia. He gave her a peck on the lips.

"Darling, after the night we've had, I need to eat."

Revolted by the exaggerated display of affection, Ava recoiled in horror. But she caught Connor's glance her way and knew he wanted to see her reaction. Probably mistaking her expression of revolt as a sign of jealousy, he gave her a self-satisfied grin.

"Shall we?" asked Nico.

"Shall we what?"

"Shall we talk?"

"No," replied Ava. "We can talk later." He always brought out the sensual side to her.

And there it was again. Her best intentions to remain as "friends only" had no hope in hell of happening.

CHAPTER TWENTY-TWO

They lay in bed, reveling in the afterglow of their messy lovemaking.

Nico smiled. Ava had initiated this, not him. She needed him; she had given him a second chance.

He would see to it that he never let her down again.

Lying there in the quietness of the pensione, a warmth radiated through the entire length of his body. Ava lay snuggled up against him and she now stared up at him, her face dewy, her eyes shining.

He turned to his side, unable to keep his hands off her body. With his fingers he traced light lines across her collarbone and heard her mewl in delight, before his hands skimmed along her arms.

She inched closer to him, moaning softly. Encouraged and with mounting excitement, his fingers disappeared beneath the sheets and sought out the smooth, soft skin of her inner thighs.

"Again?" She squealed in delight, rolling her body closer. Just as he was about to dip lower and give her another one of his deep, wet kisses, he stopped suddenly and groaned.

"Dammit. I have a meeting I need to be at." He yanked his wrist upwards and scowled at his watch.

Ava moaned in disappointment and gripped his back with her long fingers. She rolled closer against him, the soft swell of her breasts teasing his chest. Blood coursed through his veins as heat pooled in one place.

But he had to go.

The temptation before him was too great, but if he stayed and gave in, as every fiber of his body screamed at him to, he might have consequences to suffer later.

Desire or duty?

"I'm sorry," he whispered, gazing at her pensively. "I hate to leave you. Believe me, there's no other place I'd rather be." He took a moment to gaze down at her dreamy expression. Her messed up hair cascaded around her shoulders as she stared back at him seductively with her large molten eyes.

The woman had bewitched him. It was almost impossible for him to leave the bed.

"But then again," he murmured, seeing her full lips stretch out into a smile. He hovered closer towards her and the feel of her fingers just below his stomach sealed the deal. He moved over her, covering the full length of her body with his, before pressing his body against hers. He gave her a long, lingering kiss as a low groan fell from his lips.

Pulling away would be impossible.

Giving in was all there was.

Taking her now, being consumed by her, was all he could do. The scheduled phone call with the manager of the Cazale Roma could wait.

Elsa had been transported to a world of serenity and beauty, so overwhelmed was she by the Duomo, Verona's stunning cathedral.

Edmondo had chosen this as his first place of interest for them to visit. He had taken his time showing her beautiful frescoes that were hundreds of years old, and the octagonal Romanesque baptismal font carved out of a single block of marble and decorated with carved biblical scenes.

He held her spellbound with stories about the twelfth century church so elaborately crafted and filled with gems. It was architecturally beautiful from the outside and filled with a myriad of things to see inside.

It had been a most wonderful way to spend the time. Ava had been so thoughtful in planning this for her.

"Your daughter seems to be a good influence on my son," Edmondo commented, holding the door open for Elsa. They walked out of the coffee shop where they had stopped for a warm and milky latte.

"She is a good girl, my Ava, but I worry about her. She has had a bad time of things lately." They walked along the street, these two strangers who were now starting to feel at ease with one another.

"That was rather unfortunate, though I don't know the whole story. Nico has not said much about it." They continued walking at a reasonably slow pace. Elsa turned to look at him. She did not like the idea that news about her daughter's woes was being broadcast everywhere. Even if it was just to Nico's father. "It wasn't her fault."

"Of course not," Edmondo reassured her. "I see that the young man in question has chosen to follow her all the way here? Does he think there's any hope of a reconciliation?"

Elsa snorted. "He should have saved himself the air fare. You can tell what sort of a man he is. I believe he has now set his sights on someone else, a lady I often see at the hotel. A blonde-haired woman."

Edmondo coughed lightly. "Silvia."

"You know her?" she asked in surprise. Edmondo kept his eyes fixed on the street ahead. He shook his head slowly. "I know her," he answered, his voice tight. "Tell me, Elsa, are you ready to go back or would you like to see something else?"

She didn't have to think about it for too long. Edmondo was pleasant and easygoing, and it was freeing for her to have the company of someone her own age. For too long now she had felt like a third wheel. Always around to help her daughters, to be the child-minder, cook and have them all over, be there to listen to their troubles. Her girls were good; they doted on her, and they were always there for her, but as time went on and the girls became busy with their own lives, she started to feel more like an 'extra' in their lives instead of a 'part.'

Today, she felt back in touch with life. Though she had a great social life back in Denver with her group of friends, she did not have any male friends. In fact, she had never considered the idea of meeting anyone after her husband had been taken so suddenly and so shockingly from her.

Being out with a man felt different to being out with her women friends.

She wasn't looking for romance, and so this subtle friendship felt uncomplicated. Easy and simple.

Edmondo was kind and attentive in a way that was different to her women friends. She liked this new feeling as much as she liked to think that he was enjoying himself, too. If he was asking her to come and see something else, surely it implied that he was?

Who was she to refuse such an offer?

"I would love to see anything, whatever you suggest," she replied, her enthusiastic voice louder than she had intended.

"Good. There is another stunning church, the Basilica di San Zeno Maggiore, but perhaps we can do that another day."

Another day? Elsa's heart gave a little leap for joy. Edmondo was already thinking of other places to take her.

"We could go to Castelvecchio. You might like it. It is a medieval fortress, dating back to the fourteenth century and it's also a museum of art. Would you like to see it?"

Elsa's eyes shone. "I would. It sounds wonderful. Thank you."

Edmondo cleared his throat before asking, a little shyly, "And then perhaps, afterwards we could stop off somewhere and have a late lunch, or an early dinner? We'll both be hungry by then," he added. "I'm not sure how long we'll be."

She looked at him with soft eyes, sensing his shyness at asking her. Beaming a huge smile that came from deep inside, she told him, "That would be lovely."

She found herself looking forward to the rest of the day very much.

CHAPTER TWENTY-THREE

Tori wriggled in her high chair and pushed away the spoon of mashed up avocado and banana that Rona attempted to force into her mouth.

She was hungry, Rona knew it, but she was also overtired, and hungry mixed with overtired did not make for a good combination.

The trip to the airport had overexcited her, with the rush of people and the wonders of being in a new and unfamiliar place. It had not helped that Carlos had gotten her overexcited by messing around with her constantly. He was going to miss his little girl. Tori had cried, holding onto to his neck for dear life as he said goodbye and left to board his flight.

"Stop that!" Rona snapped. Tori slammed her hand down on a spoonful of food. Globs of slimy green gunk smudged everywhere, including on Rona's face.

Enjoying the effect she had just caused, Tori banged her fist on the table before Rona slammed down the plastic feeding bowl and wiped the little girl's hands clean.

Rona was not at all amused. Damn Carlos for leaving.

And damn his father, too. The old man could easily have gotten another person to help at the restaurant. Carlos had only been gone a couple of hours and already she was exhausted.

The easy sound of laughter drew her attention and she looked away from the bunch of tissues smeared with green, to see her mother and Nico's father walking in, looking the perfect picture of contentment.

Rona stared at them in disbelief as she looked from Elsa's flushed and happy face to Edmondo's relaxed one. He looked at ease, and so did her mother.

"Mom?"

"Hi, honey."

Tori perked up and made a giggly noise as Grandma straight towards her.

"Did Carlos get off all right?"

Carlos was the last thing on her mind. Rona sat forward and furiously scrubbed the highchair's feeding table, needing something to do. She waved her hand, dismissing her husband completely. "Are you having a nice day, Mom?" She glanced at Edmondo and tried to soften her words with a smile.

"I've had a wonderful day, thanks to Mr. Cazale." Elsa beamed at him, her face aglow.

Edmondo dismissed her remarks graciously. "It was *I* who had a wonderful time. It is always a great thrill to show Verona to visitors. I love to see it for the first time through their eyes."

"We visited the Duomo and then Castelvecchio in the afternoon," her mother told her, excitement turning her voice higher. Rona pursed her lips together tightly, trying to keep her words under control.

As if sensing that there was about to be some sort of

family dispute, Edmondo turned to Elsa, thanked her for her lovely company, excused himself and left.

"He even offered to drop me to the door. Such a gentleman. I can see where his son gets his manners from." Elsa sat down across the table from Rona. "Can I take her?" she asked, squeezing Tori's chubby little hand gently.

"I wish you had been around to take her earlier. I'm shattered. Now that Carlos is gone, this isn't going to be much of a holiday for me."

Elsa lifted her granddaughter out of the highchair and hugged her to her chest, planting a big kiss on her cheek, then sat down with her on her lap, completely avoiding Rona's comments.

"Mom!" Rona all but stamped her foot petulantly. Elsa looked up calmly. Rona met her mother's cool gaze and was immediately at a loss for words.

"You really should visit the Duomo sometime. It's a beautiful building." Elsa smiled at Tori who had snuggled up against her chest. She was sleepy and curled herself up into her grandmother's comforting body.

Rona started tapping her feet on the floor. "Shall we get something to eat? Maybe go back to that little restaurant in town?"

Elsa stifled a yawn. "We ate on the way back."

"You did?"

"Yes, we walked so much. We were so hungry at the end and Edmondo wanted to take me to a little restaurant near the fortress."

"You and *Edmondo*?" Rona crossed her arms.

"That's right," Elsa replied calmly.

Rona's eyes narrowed and she grew irritable the more Elsa talked. "Sure, you go ahead, Mom. You take a nap, and maybe tomorrow we'll do some sightseeing of our own."

"I'm not sure what my plans are for tomorrow," Elsa said, a little hesitantly. She kissed her granddaughter and handed her back to Rona. "Tori looks as though she's going to fall asleep any second now. Put her to bed, honey. It might be a good idea for you to get some rest too. You look a little tired yourself."

Rona stared at her mother, speechless.

"Goodnight, honey," Elsa called as she toddled off for a good night of rest.

CHAPTER TWENTY-FOUR

"You're smiling again," said Ava.

"I can't help it." Nico kissed her fingers before wrapping his hand around hers. They were walking back from having dinner. The long, delicious afternoon of their reunion had crept toward the evening and the sky was a dark plum-colored purple by the time they left the restaurant to return home.

He felt so light and carefree that he would have jogged back from the restaurant if Ava had let him. The tension that had gnarled itself into a ball around his neck and shoulders for days had all but melted away.

The effect she had on him intrigued him more each day and he hated that they'd wasted over a week keeping their distance.

"I wonder where my father took your mother?" He remembered what had brought him back to Ava this morning.

"My Mom would have loved it no matter where they went. She's enjoying her time here. I believe she already loves Verona as much as I do."

Nico slipped his fingers out of her hand and encircled her

waist, drawing her closer to him. "And what is it that you love about Verona?" he asked, kissing her quickly on the lips as she looked up at him.

"The buildings, the food, the Duomo."

"Is that all?"

"The pasta, the wine, the seafood, the restaurants."

"Anything else?"

"The hotels, the service, the culture."

"Nothing else?"

Ava cocked her head to the side, pretending to think, then opened her mouth to make an announcement and closed her lips tight, just as quickly. "No, nothing else." She forced away the smirk that had started to settle on her lips.

"Nothing else. I see." He nodded slowly, playing along. They reached her door and Ava turned the key and walked in, expecting Nico to follow. When he didn't, she gave him a quizzical look.

"Aren't you coming in?" She cocked her head and raising a beautifully plucked eyebrow. His hesitation seemed to get the better of her curiosity. "Nico?"

"I've got an early morning meeting tomorrow." He hesitated, finding himself caught up between his strong desire for her and logical reasoning that instructed him to deal with urgent business matters. "I should go." He had already overridden his logical mind's reasoning once today.

Disappointment washed over Ava's face. "Are you sure? We don't have to—"

"I know." He leaned in and kissed her lightly on the lips, as if the very touch of her would be enough to ensnare him again.

"We could talk, have a cup of coffee." She smiled at him provocatively.

He looked down at his shoes, trying to fight the

temptation. He couldn't resist her, not with those eyes and those lips. Forcing his eyes closed, he summoned up the willpower to move away and stepped back.

Now that things were good between them again, his mind was freer and the possibilities he saw for his future presented themselves easily. He still had to visit the Cazale hotels, bring each one up to his standard so that they matched the Casa Adriana in terms of excellence and customer experience. Ava had been here the entire month, and now that he admitted it to himself, he had held off carrying out this task because he hadn't wanted to be away from her.

Throughout dinner he had been formulating a plan. Now that fate had allowed her a few more weeks here, it seemed perfect. All he needed was for Ava to say 'yes'.

Against the backdrop of the darkened purple night sky, his heart thudded furiously. He wanted to ask her to come with him, but he didn't want to frighten her off either. He understood her well enough now to know that talk of a commitment or anything which signified that might make her run the other way. They only had a little time left. He couldn't afford not to try.

"I'm leaving for a business trip tomorrow. I'll be gone three days." He paused for her reaction.

"Oh," she sounded surprised, "why don't you come inside and tell me all about it, then. It's silly to be discussing this on the doorstep."

"I've been..." He paused, his eyes narrowing. "I shouldn't have missed that meeting. You know I have this ... complicated relationship with my father. We don't always see eye to eye."

She brushed her hand lightly across his arm. "I've watched the two of you together. I understand how difficult it must be for you sometimes, but perhaps your father is hard on you because he loves you so much."

He breathed a sigh of relief. This woman understood him. Unlike anyone he had ever known, save his mother, Ava calmed him. She eased his tension and made him feel better about the rough and bumpy turn his life seemed to have taken recently.

"Why don't you come with me? It would be like a little break, just the two of us. I want to make the most of the time we have left before you return to Denver." He had much to prove to her; it wasn't just to his father.

Seeing her standing there in the doorway, with the hallway light behind her highlighting her hair, this would be a picture of her he would never forget. If she was surprised by his request, she hid it well. He tried to read her expression, but it was impassive, and she gave nothing away.

Finally, she said, "Okay," and beamed a beautiful smile at him. She hadn't even asked him where they were going.

A surge of irrepressible joy burst inside him. Three days with her all to himself. "Great."

"Are you sure about taking me along for a business meeting?"

"I'm sure," he answered easily and calmly, fighting the urge to do a victory dance.

"Why did you wait until the very end to ask me?"

He shrugged his shoulders. "I didn't want to frighten you off."

"You won't frighten me off," she said, "unless another one of your past girlfriends turns up." She jested with him, but there was an element of realism in her words.

He shook his head. "I don't intend to ever hurt you, not if I can help it."

A hint of a smile crept back on her face. "So, where are we going?"

"To visit one of the Cazale hotels in Riccione and to see another hotel nearby. I'll be busy in meetings, but I'll have time to spend with you."

Ava's smile widened. Suddenly she stepped out and laid her palms flat against his chest. "I'm looking forward to it already."

Just feeling the heat of her body close to him was enough to get him aroused again. When she then leaned in and gave him a long, lingering kiss, a kiss that promised much more, he reluctantly pulled away.

"Ava," he whispered. "You tempt me beyond all reason, but I really must go and prepare." He tortured himself a moment longer by running his fingers gently down her face while his feet remained rooted to the ground, unable to move away.

"Go now. Leave, if you must." She shooed him away with a flourish of her hand. "What time are we going tomorrow?"

But he didn't move an inch. "Late afternoon. I didn't even ask you if you had any plans for the next three days, what with your mom and sister still here."

"My family can keep themselves suitably occupied for a few days." She winked at him.

That was the kind of answer he liked to hear. Maybe, just maybe, there was time to show her that what they had was worth keeping. He cupped her cheek softly with the palm of his hand. "Pack some light clothes. Goodnight." He left her without a final kiss, leaving her wanting.

Three days alone with Ava would be heaven.

CHAPTER TWENTY-FIVE

Going to Riccione, on the eastern coast, was a welcome break for them both. Nico didn't mind the drive. He didn't mind anything much, as long as Ava was with him.

He had worked hard during the early morning to tie up all loose ends. The call he had missed with Matteo, the manager of the Cazale Roma in Rome, had been one of the loose ends. But although Nico had called him a number of times, he'd been unable to get a hold of him. He concluded that it was nothing urgent. Nothing that couldn't wait a few more days.

His father hadn't mentioned anything either.

They set off after he had tied up a few loose ends at the Casa Adriana and they arrived in the Cazale Riccione just in time for lunch. The hotel manager greeted them enthusiastically, almost tripping over himself to please Nico, his boss. He ingratiated himself with Ava, believing her to be of some importance since she was with Nico.

They had just finished a sumptuous and decadent lunch; one which was too rich for Nico's tastes. The staff were doing their best to please him.

"How do you manage all your hotels?" asked Ava, laying down her napkin.

"My father takes care of it mostly. He'll pay a visit to each hotel once every two months or so. But he has regular meetings by phone. He loves the idea of web conferencing, though he still needs to physically go and check out each place. He has to see the books, talk to the staff, inspect the property. Luckily, most of the managers he has hired are excellent."

"Eight hotels? That sounds like a lot of work."

"They're small though. And they're not in busy locations or anything. My father never liked the idea of those big, towering concrete blocks next to other buildings that were more of the same."

"He has excellent business acumen."

"He does." These smaller boutique style hotels, which was what the Cazale hotels were, were more highly sought after these days. Most especially by affluent travelers who balked at the very idea of last-minute cheap deals and the coupon culture. Being smaller, they were also easier to manage.

"This is the second of your father's hotels that I've seen and I'm already in love with them all. Your father has been so successful. No wonder he has such high expectations of you."

Nico jumped. She had it spot on. He hoped that the stop at Ravenna, on the way back, would help him gain a foothold onto the hotel property ladder. He wanted to prove, especially to himself, that he was capable and business minded, too.

"It's getting harder as time goes on. Competitors are springing up everywhere. We have lots to do to stay ahead but my father wants to slow down now, especially this last year. I have ideas and getting my father to see eye to eye with me can be challenging at best."

"But if he's worked hard to build all of this up, it's only natural that he'll want to slow down now. I can't imagine it being easy for him to let go of the business easily."

"He seems quick enough to put out that he is willing to sell, for the right price," Nico shot back.

"Maybe it's his way of testing you. Of seeing if you are up to the mark," Ava offered.

He shrugged. Whatever the reason, he was determined to show his father just how capable he was. "I'll be busy for the rest of the afternoon," he said apologetically.

Ava smiled at him. "You go ahead and do what you need to. The drive down here was breathtaking. I'm so happy that I got to see a part of Italy that I might not have seen otherwise."

"We're here for two nights. Tomorrow I should have finished most of my review of this place. I'll be able to spend more time with you then." Riccione, being the smallest of the hotels seemed a good one to roll out his hotel blueprint to. If it worked here, he knew he had a system that could be rolled out to the other hotels. But that wasn't the only reason he had come to this part of Italy.

"Two nights?" she asked, her voice husky.

"Two nights," he confirmed.

The heat between them was obvious.

His meeting with the manager was straightforward enough and he'd managed to go through the processes he wanted to implement at the Cazale Riccione in the coming months.

The staff were quick starters and loyal and, if anything went wrong, Nico would know what had to be improved before he rolled the process out elsewhere. He and Gina had worked through the plans in meticulous detail, with him overseeing matters and Gina ensuring that each process was carried out to the letter.

Their attempts to improve the customer experience and increase the quality of their service had gone extremely well at the Casa Adriana. If he could now implement the same process at the Cazale Riccione—and it proved successful— he'd have a blueprint for the other hotels. This was how he planned to bring all the other hotels to the same level of excellence.

By the time he'd detailed his vision and put proper milestones in place, it was late evening. He was anxious to get the bulk of the meetings out of the way today, so that there was only little required of him tomorrow.

He was eager to spend most of the day with Ava; he needed to make it up to her. He'd dragged her all the way out here and then left her all alone and it made him feel guilty even though she'd been more than happy to come along with him.

Now that their recent separation was behind them, they'd fallen into an easy camaraderie again. It was almost like how it used to be during their time in Venice.

Nothing would ruin things now.

He carried out the inspection of the kitchens and the rest of the hotel building and by the time he finished, he was relieved the day was over. Suitably happy that he had achieved what he had set out to do, he returned to his room.

Ava had fallen asleep and beside her lay a magazine thrown open along the middle. There were photos of him at a Grand Prix party, taken alongside famous racing car drivers and beautiful women. The article was in English, which meant Ava had read it all.

He sighed, shaking his head in anger. Even on a trip away,

these things haunted him. He lay down beside her and watched her sleeping.

The last thing he wanted to do was to hurt this woman.

———

Light fingers tickled her face, and Ava stirred. She was a light sleeper at the best of times. Stretching out, she flickered her eyes open a little. Her gaze fell on Nico's face, and she smiled.

His eyes never left her face, but she could tell that he was tired and a little tense. "What's wrong?" she asked, sensing his unease.

"This." He held up the magazine so that she faced the full page spread. Ava looked from the magazine to his eyes peering just above it. This wonderful man was doing his best to make everything perfect and right for her.

She flicked the magazine away, at the same time annoyed with herself for falling asleep.

"You looked so ridiculously boyish back then." She pointed to the photos.

His perplexed face spoke volumes. She moved in closer to him, enjoying his look of surprise. "I prefer the more mature, manlier version of you now."

His lips turned up and relief flooded his features, wiping away the tension that had crept in. It was obvious that he'd been worried about her response. She didn't want him to worry any more. It was an old magazine.

Why the hotel had kept this she didn't know. She'd found it buried deep below the pile of magazines on one of the tables and had brought it up to read.

"You're not angry?" he asked, looking at her lips. She reacted by licking hers.

"About what? The 'rich and handsome' Nico Cazale? Or

the 'playboy heartthrob' who leaves a 'trail of broken hearts' wherever he goes? Or the 'Romeo hunk' who has no trouble finding women?" Ava reeled off phrases verbatim from the article. She couldn't blame him for things that had happened in his past, no more than he could blame her for anything in hers.

They were equal now and if there was a chance of anything further growing between them, she had to learn to deal with things from his past.

Nico feigned a bored expression. "This is boring. It's old news. They're talking about someone else, of course." He moved off the bed in one smooth movement and removed his tie.

It was when he started unbuttoning his shirt that excitement danced in her veins.

"I'm taking a shower and then I'm taking you to dinner," he promised. His mood was instantly elevated and his eyes shone with promise.

"How about something in between?" She lay on the bed like a seductive temptress, wanting him to see what type of 'something' she had in mind.

He tossed off his shirt and walked over to her, a fire in his gaze as he bent down and kissed her hungrily. "Don't move," he warned her and walked away, leaving her to admire his smooth, broad, naked back.

CHAPTER TWENTY-SIX

Ava was happy, tired happy, sleep-deprived happy. Happy.

Time alone with Nico made her giddy. Being away from the hectic demands of Nico's work as well as the demands of her family meant they only had eyes for each other.

They hadn't made it out of the room last night and had ordered room service instead.

The next day Nico had inspected the hotel and the kitchens and spoken to all the members of staff individually, his job had been done.

He had taken Ava out to what he referred to as one of his favorite places, out in the beauty and quiet of the countryside and the hills of Riccione.

Even though the Cazale Riccione was situated away from the trawling, sprawling, buzzing nightclubs, restaurants and nightlife of Riccione, where most of the tourists went, he had taken her out farther. It wasn't until she was high up in the hills that she had realized how much quieter and off the beaten path most of his favorite places were.

In a quaint little restaurant, they ate culatello, the prized white truffle, drank good wine and enjoyed a hearty meal.

They stayed on at the restaurant, until even the kitchen staff had cleared up and were ready to go home. Then they drove back to the hotel and talked some more, into the early hours of the morning.

And then, when they were too tired to do anything else but fall asleep, they did so—happy and full from the good things that life had to offer—in each other's arms.

When they left Riccione, it was with a wonderful picture book of memories. Here, where there had been no one else but the two of them, it had given her an idea of what life could be like, might be like, should anything further develop between them.

If she wasn't careful, he would take her heart forever.

On their drive back to Verona, Nico stopped off along the way. Ava was grateful to get out and stretch her legs. She shut the car door behind her and stifled a yawn. "Is this another one of your hotels?" She stared up at the slightly shabby-looking white building in front of them.

"I don't know." Nico scratched his chin and slipped his other hand around hers. "You tell me." He cocked his head, waiting for an answer.

"I don't understand." Nico wasn't making any sense.

"Then follow me." He pulled her along with him and walked into the hotel.

"Mr. Cazale." An impeccably dressed man held out his hand and greeted them.

Ava looked around her at the big lobby area, with its peeling wallpaper that exposed dank, stained walls, and faded curtains with falling swags. It may have been decadent once, but now it looked worn and weary.

"What are we doing here?" she whispered, nudging in

closer towards him as they followed the sharp-suited man around.

Nico waved his hand at the man who had been speaking to him in Italian and gave her his full attention. "What do you think of this place?"

"It's nice...a bit shabby and it's empty."

"I'm thinking of buying it. It has potential."

"This place?" She looked at it with new eyes. Nico nodded and waved to the man who stood patiently waiting for them, signifying that he needed a moment more.

He let go of her hand and walked around, excitement dancing in his eyes. "This place has potential. It's been on the market for a while, but I can already see how we could bring this in line with the Casa Adriana. It's a risk, but not too big a risk. It's near the coast, but away from the other cheap and cheerful hotels. I can already see in my mind's eye how beautiful it could be. I see it as more than just a hotel, this would be perfect as a spa retreat, offering treatments. A complete sanctuary for indulgence."

"I'd stay here," said Ava excitedly, she could see the possibilities he was painting. "I know you could make this work, Nico. But do you think buying a new hotel is the thing to do right now, when you have so many other hotels to look after already? A new place would put so much extra pressure on you. Maybe you could wait a while?" His face dropped a little at her reply. She didn't want to dissuade him, but he had asked her opinion. He wanted to prove himself but to do so at the cost of working himself to death would be wrong. She added, "I believe you can do this, but you need to make sure it's for the right reasons."

"I'm all for looking after my father's hotels, and maintaining and improving them, but I need to do something by myself. Something from the beginning. I've been lucky that my father built up his empire, but sometimes, people look at me and think I was given everything easily. That I have it all made."

"Do it because you want to do it, but don't make yourself ill by taking too much on. Besides, you shouldn't worry about what people think. You don't need to do it to prove anything to others. Or to your father."

"I'm doing it for us. I mean—" His face reddened.

"Us? Nico, I—" She hesitated. This little break had been a culmination of things; it had allowed her to begin to believe that they could become more. They had touched upon these very things in their late night, early morning pillow talks. But with Nico saying it out aloud in the cold light of day, her panic started to seep in. And when he didn't say anything, she still panicked.

What did she want?

He rushed to soothe her. "I meant my father and me."

Now it was her turn to blush. "Oh. Okay." She felt silly. "It's a beautiful building." She walked away, pointing around at the walls and high ceilings, anything, to detract from what she had just assumed.

"Shall we look around?" He offered her his arm, and she gladly took it.

Though she put on a brave face, Ava wondered what a future in Italy with Nico would be like.

CHAPTER TWENTY-SEVEN

Nico sat in his car and allowed himself the indulgence of remembering.

They'd arrived back late last night and this morning, leaving Ava's bed had been nothing short of torture.

Spending each night together again, on their short break away, had been something he had missed.

In the space of a few years, he had gone from a man with a different woman each week, to one who had bouts of short-lived celibacy, give or take the odd woman who caught his eye. Now here he was, reveling in the very picture of sweet cosiness and with a woman who did not seem so eager to commit. The irony of it.

Apart from that week when they had argued, he had barely slept at his home since their return from Venice. The more time he spent with Ava, the more he knew he wanted more of it. And now he had a sense that she was starting to feel about him the way he had been feeling about her.

The one thing he didn't want to be was a rebound relationship: the bridging gap between a bad mistake and the stepping stone to better things.

He stayed in his car, not quite ready to jump back into a hectic day of work. His mind distracted by the three glorious days he had spent with the woman who now occupied a permanent place in his heart and mind.

What would he do when she left?

He had deliberately not broached this topic, had not dared to ask her about her future plans. He knew what he wanted. What he was less certain of was how to go about getting it. He felt that she was starting to be as committed as he was. A couple of times the words had slipped from her mouth, about her wanting to stay on here. She had toyed with the idea of spending a few months in Verona and a few months in the US. She had justified it by saying she needed to buy more merchandise, though they both knew it wasn't the real reason.

Ava was starting to feel something for him, and he just had to be patient.

It had to come from her first.

With a tightening chest, he pulled himself out of his car and prepared for a day of meetings and business calls. He had to focus on the business. Otherwise, thoughts of Ava's imminent departure would only tear him up.

It was early, after six o'clock in the morning and the hotel desk was unmanned. Nico rushed to his office, but the sound of a sneeze coming from his father's office froze him in place.

Nico knew his father was an early bird, but six o'clock? Whatever was he doing here?

He knocked and entered. His father looked up, barely batting an eyelid, his face as calm as ever. Even the sight of Nico arriving at the office this early, did not faze him.

"Good morning, Papa." Nico was enthusiastic, and ready to take on the world this morning.

"Good business trip?" Edmondo asked.

The corners of Nico's mouth turned up slightly. "Most definitely, Papa."

"And this visit to Riccione, was it urgent?"

Nico didn't see where this was going. "I had it arranged. It was in the diary. I told you I was going to roll out our new process at the Cazale Riccione."

"The conference call with Matteo from the Cazale Roma was also arranged and in the diary. But you managed to miss that." The old man dove straight in.

By now, Nico guessed that something of great importance had happened, or, more likely, gone wrong at the Cazale Roma. This was his father's way of letting him know he had messed up big time.

"I know I missed the call, Papa, but I rang the next day and Matteo wasn't available. You weren't around for me to tell you." It had been the call he missed when he'd gone to Ava's pensione and they had made up; the day Edmondo had showed Elsa around Verona.

Nico eyed his father and waited for him to drop the bomb. He noticed his father was dressed casually, too. No shirt, tie or business suit today. Instead, he wore a pair of slacks and a short-sleeved shirt.

The old man clasped his hands together and rested them on his stomach. He waited for Nico to elaborate.

"Tell me what went wrong? Apart from me missing the call, Papa?" The exuberance he had felt about telling his father of his news vanished into the air. He felt his energy drain to the very soles of his feet.

"Because you failed to do something you considered trivial, the situation which could have been contained, had you known of it, has now blown up."

It had only been a routine weekly meeting with the hotel manager. Why was his father making such a big deal of it all?

Nico felt like a young child summoned to his father's study, needing to explain yet again why his test marks had not been as good as they should have been.

Yet he could hardly blame his father. In truth, Nico should not have put pleasure before business. He should have taken the call when it was scheduled, even if it was just a normal call.

"They've had problems with the staff at the Cazale Roma. A dispute between Matteo and the head chef has escalated out of control. The head chef has walked out and the rest of the staff are up in arms. And they have nobody heading up the kitchen."

Nico's muscles tensed.

"You failed to do something I asked you to do. And then not only do you fail to attend, you fail to follow things up later. Your actions have consequences." His father unlocked his hands and busied himself with some paperwork on his desk; the mere action of being ignored was the one thing Nico hated the most. Unfortunately, it was something his father was very good at.

He swallowed. "I'm sorry, Papa." Once more he felt like the small child who always sought his father's approval. But this time he really had messed up. Problems had erupted in Rome, something out of his control and not in any way related to the usual weekly conference call. A missed weekly conference call would not have been such a big deal. Losing the head chef, however, and having unrest among the workers was another problem. A much bigger problem. His father was justifiably angry.

"And you expect me to designate responsibility to you for running these hotels?" His father looked through his paperwork with concentration again.

"I'll get onto it right away," Nico offered. The meetings he had planned for looking into the legal and property issues for the hotel in Ravenna would have to be put on hold, for now. It might not be a good time to tell his father about that hotel just yet.

"Of course you will get onto it. Maybe if you hadn't completely forgotten about the call, unrelated as it was to the problem we currently have on our hands, we might have prevented this fallout."

He turned to leave and then stood his ground. Perhaps it *was* better to tell him now and then deal with the mess of the Cazale Roma. "There's a hotel in Ravenna I've looked at. It has a lot of potential." He waited for a response.

Sure enough the older man immediately stopped what he was doing. Nico waited for the backlash, the questions, the sting in the tail, the one where his father would point out something obviously wrong and make him feel this small again.

Only it never happened. He blinked and in that instant, he wasn't sure if what he saw in his father's eyes was a gleam of admiration. Edmondo sat back again. "A hotel, eh?" Was that a touch of pride that he detected in his father's voice?

The shock of not getting an interrogation or having to prove himself, as he was usually required, startled Nico.

"We'd gone out to visit the Cazale Riccione, but I'd had my eye on a hotel near Ravenna that had been put up for sale a while back."

"Two Cazale hotels that close to one another?" Edmondo sounded unsure.

"I know how it seems, but listen to me, Papa. This hotel has a lot of land. It's at a good price. We could turn it into something a bit more exclusive. Make it a spa retreat, a relaxation par excellence, not just a place to sleep for the night. But a center for peace and tranquility."

The old man guffawed. "You read too many business books. Sometimes people just want a place to sleep for the night. It's how I built my empire. By giving them exactly what they needed. Not by trying to sell them something they might not want, let alone need."

Nico was already prepared for this reaction. He had fought these battles every step of the way. "Spa resorts are big business."

Edmondo pressed his lips together. He didn't look convinced.

"Of course, you'll have to see it first, Papa." It would be the best way of easing his father's reluctance. If his father could only see what Nico saw in it. And what Ava had come to see once he had told her his vision. "We loved it as soon as we saw it."

"We?"

"Ava. I asked her to come along with me."

"Ah."

"But I'm sure you must know that because, according to Ava, you've been showing her mother around these past few days."

His father's ears turned red. It was a reaction that Nico didn't recall seeing before. What had happened to him in a few days? Nico felt more emboldened than ever. "The hotel is in a fantastic location, but most people won't be keen on it because it's far from the main center. But you know our hotels always do so well because we don't cater to the masses." He appealed directly to his father's business sense. "For a spa retreat, it's perfect. Ava loved it."

The old man snorted.

"That's not why I think it has potential," Nico said quickly.

"I should hope not." When it came to business, his father

only had a business head on. Nothing and no one else influenced his choices.

"It was good to get another perspective on the place, but I would have been interested in it anyway, even if Ava hadn't been there." Nico waited for the questions, the price, the legal issues, the timelines, the plan going forward, the estimates, the full business case proposal. But his father did not demand any of these things. Instead, he nodded his head in a gesture that almost bordered on approval.

"I can see that you are very enthusiastic about the plans for this new hotel. I would like to see it for myself at some point soon."

"Of course, Papa." Could it really be that his father was at last pleased about a business move he had just made? Nico realized it was the biggest and boldest move he had ever made. "Don't you want to know anything?" Nico asked, fearing his father was just playing along with him. He was still waiting for the bite in the back. For a second he wondered if his father was feeling ill. "Are you feeling all right, Papa?"

"I'm feeling very well."

Nico was perplexed. It was still early morning. Perhaps his father had plans for the day. Remembering the day trip with Ava's mother, he asked him, "How was your day when you showed Elsa around?"

"Very enjoyable." The old man looked up and Nico swore that his father's eyes were laughing. "We've been on excursions every day, actually. Elsa is so appreciative of everything, it's hard not to want to show her more places."

Was it possible that Ava's mother was the reason his father was in such a good mood?

"She seems to be a nice enough woman," Nico commented. He wasn't sure what to make of his father's new friendship.

"She is," his father agreed. "You seem to be taken with her daughter."

"I am." The corners of Nico's lips turned up slightly, and he gave his father a funny look. He wasn't ready yet to tell his father just how taken he was with Ava. All things in good time.

"You didn't tell me what you were going to do to resolve the problem at the Cazale Roma."

"I'll call Matteo now and find out what's going on." Nico made to leave. He would get the call out of the way, see if he could resolve this problem quickly. He was anxious to get to his office and draw up projections for the proposed new hotel. If his father liked it and they decided to move forward, it was going to be a huge project, and he would need to assemble a team to inspect the building, not to mention the whole raft of legal issues that needed to be dealt with. There was also financing to be worked out. He would need to prepare for everything.

But before any of that could take place he needed his father's approval, for the only person who could help with the financing was sitting in front of him, watching him carefully.

"A word of advice, Nico. Staff problems can erupt and fester if not dealt with. And they are the very problems that cannot be rectified easily over the phone."

Nico had a sinking feeling his father had already planned his schedule for him. "What exactly do you propose?"

"You're booked on the seven thirty flight to Rome this evening. Matteo is expecting you."

Back in his own office, Nico collapsed into his chair and let out a huge sigh, but the pressure building up inside him failed to release. He had messed up, and he had to fix it. And his father was going to make sure he did.

He had planned to see Ava this evening, but now he

wasn't even going to be around. His father didn't say how long he needed to be away, but Nico intended to be back as soon as possible.

He flicked through his desk diary with irritation. He had a meeting with a journalist from one of the travel magazines in a few hours' time. He shook his head; it was one more thing he could do without.

Still, if it was publicity for the hotel, he might as well see her.

CHAPTER TWENTY-EIGHT

Ava yawned and stretched out lazily in bed, letting her hands slide across the silky white sheets.

Memories of the past few days with Nico set her pulse racing. She couldn't contain her smile any more than she could help settle the funny feeling inside her. They had reached a better understanding of one another and things were back to normal again. But better. Deeper.

There was no way around it: she'd fallen for him, hard. No matter her resolve to be careful and take things slowly; there was no slow when it came to Nico. Yet they terrified her, the strength of her feelings for him.

She couldn't remember ever feeling this way before, for anyone. Their days together had cemented one thing for them both—there was a possibility that what they had could grow into something more. He had alluded to it. He would look at her sometimes as though he wanted to say something, and she wondered if he would ever say those three little words that she now ached to hear. But he never did. And as much as they were on the tip of her tongue, she couldn't bring herself to say them, not until she heard them from him first.

And if they said those words to one another, then what? What if she stayed here? It *could* work. Flitting between here and Denver.

She stretched out again, but the tiredness she felt was overwhelming, even though she had slept well. She lay under the sheets and relived some of the intimate moments they had shared these last few days. A slow, steady warmth spread out all over her body as she hungered to have him in her arms again.

How he had managed to get to work this morning, she had no idea. She could barely get herself out of bed.

Nico told her to stay in today, to take it easy, and that he would come and see her after work. She knew he had a busy day ahead of him. He didn't say it, but she could sense his trepidation about returning to work. He needed to report back to his father and the new hotel they had seen was foremost in his mind. What his father thought of him mattered more than he cared to admit.

His father seemed to be a nice enough man; he had been welcoming and generous with her when he had offered to show her mother the delights of Verona, but she could see that he was hard on his son. Somehow it felt as though his father was testing Nico and needed confirmation, as she had, that his playboy days were long gone.

She knew that dealing with his wealth and his past, which always seemed to show up in his present, was not something she handled too well, but for his sake she would try. She had tried when she'd seen the magazine at the Cazale Riccione. It hadn't been too difficult, now that she had dropped her preconceived notions about him.

The Nico she now knew was full of tenderness and so much love for her.

Consumed as she was by thoughts of him, she knew she

couldn't stay in bed any longer. She burst out of bed, but then slowed right down again. The tiredness hadn't completely gone, and she took her time getting ready.

As she stepped out into the bright and fresh mid-morning sun, she wondered about checking in on her mother and Rona next door. She might end up there for hours. She would surprise them later, maybe even spend the day with them. But first she needed to see Nico, even if that meant blatantly ignoring his suggestion to stay at home and get some rest.

How could she rest when nearly every thought, every waking moment was filled with him?

As she approached the hotel doors, the sight before her immediately arrested her: Edmondo Cazale and her mother were heading toward her and from the looks of things they were going out together again.

Her mother's cheeks were flushed a slight tinge of pink. Was that a new pair of trousers? Or was it that her mother's appearance looked completely different now? The deep wrinkles were still there, but Elsa had a more animated look about her. In fact, she looked radiant.

What was going on?

Her mother said something, then Edmondo laughed, and her mother laughed, too. Ava watched entranced.

The doors flew open and Edmondo and Elsa tumbled out. "You're back!" Her mother reached out and hugged her daughter, kissing her on the cheek.

"Mom?" Ava's hands rested lightly on her mother's shoulders. It had only been a few days since she had last seen her, but her mother had an effervescence about her that made Ava do a double take.

"You're glowing. How was your trip?" her mother asked.

"Riccione was beautiful." Ava nodded her head, acknowledging Edmondo as she answered.

"Ah, yes. She is right. The eastern Riviera has a bit of everything, the sea and countryside," said Edmondo.

"Where are you going today?" Ava asked her mother. She was going to add—but didn't—that they could spend some time together this afternoon. Her mother was evidently too busy.

Edmondo answered for Elsa. "I thought I would show your mother the Basilica di San Zeno Maggiore today."

"I guess that's where we're going." Elsa turned to Edmondo with a smile.

"And maybe lunch somewhere around the Piazza delle Erbe. You would like that, too, Elsa. Or we can go to that other restaurant you like so much. It's up to you."

"Edmondo knows all the restaurant owners," her mother said, her eyes twinkling. "We always get the nicest tables with some lovely views."

The way they talked to one another made Ava look twice. Her mother emanated happiness. They seemed so at ease together that Ava felt like a gooseberry standing in their way. It was a sight she would never have imagined she would be seeing.

Elsa had never been with anyone else since they had lost their father so suddenly. It had never occurred to Ava that she would ever see her mother with another man. Now to find her responding to the charms of Edmondo Cazale made her feel a little uncomfortable.

She felt the sudden need to talk to her mother, to have her to herself for the day. But her mother had other plans.

"The driver has arrived. Shall we go?" Edmondo glanced out toward the car park and nodded his head at the young man who stood discreetly by his car. Ava glanced over her shoulder. They had hired a car to take them around for the day.

"Where's Rona?" Ava blurted out, wanting to talk about something different. She felt a mixture of guilt and shame for feeling bad when she should have felt happy for her mom. She couldn't understand why she felt the way she did. She hadn't seen her mother look so light and cheery in years. It was as if she had suddenly lost ten years in age overnight. So why did she feel so unsure about it all?

"Rona's at home with Tori. The baby kept her up most of the night so she's having a lie-in."

Ava squeezed her mother's thin hand. "Don't worry, we'll catch up when you get back." She summoned up the courage to give her mother and Edmondo a comforting smile.

Ava stared at the car as it crept out of the hotel driveway. She cut a solitary figure alone on the steps of the hotel.

Knowing that Nico was inside cheered her up instantly. She could not wait to look into those deep brown eyes or to feel his soft lips against hers. Perhaps she could convince him to come back to the pensione early.

With the day's mission decided, she headed into the hotel, knowing that the tall, dark and gorgeous businessman would be working hard behind his desk. She knocked quickly and entered, not waiting for his permission.

But the scene she interrupted slashed her to the core, as though a knife had sliced right through her body. She stumbled back in shock, squeezing her eyes shut, shutting the image out. It was as if she had been punched in the face, seeing Nico, with his body up against a woman's, his hands around her wrists. The smug look of pleasure on the woman's face clawed at Ava's eyes.

By the time Nico turned his head to see her, she'd stepped back out and closed the door. His angry expression told her everything. She'd caught him red-handed and there was no way he could talk himself out of this one.

Her already uneasy stomach churned, and a rancid taste shot up her throat. She knew she was going to throw up. Spinning on her heels, she rushed to the rest room just outside the dining area and heaved violently into the toilet.

This was no photo, no lies printed on paper, no story that could be easily explained away. She had seen it with her own eyes. This was the truth of it all.

The man could not be trusted and he would never change.

How blind and stupid had she been to even think there could ever be anything between them?

Ava wiped away traces of vomit and pulled down the toilet cover. She sat down and almost at once, the floodgates opened.

Sobs exploded from deep in her body. She clutched her hand to her chest, but it was too late. The damage had already been done.

CHAPTER TWENTY-NINE

When she was sure she no longer looked like a complete train wreck, even though her heart had been bulldozed to the ground, and when she had nothing left in her stomach to throw up, Ava forced herself to leave the safety of the rest room.

She never wanted to see Nico again; she couldn't stomach any more lies. She had half expected him to run after her, to put forth his version of events. When he hadn't, she knew this was proof enough of his guilt.

She had to get away from here. She had to go home.

Peeking her head out, she saw that the lobby was clear. Even Gina was nowhere to be seen. Bile threatened to rise in her throat again, bringing up the feelings of betrayal. She took a deep breath to calm her nerves. Her desire to leave was overwhelming. Exhaling slowly, she tiptoed across the lobby, desperate to get distance between her and this hotel. And that man. She flung open the glass doors and almost tumbled down the stairs in her haste.

"Haven't seen you in a while, Ava." For the first time in a long time, Ava was relieved to hear that voice. Connor stood on the steps, leaning back against the handrail. She immediately came to a standstill.

"You don't look so good. What's wrong?" He seemed genuine in his concern for her, and she needed to throw him off the trail. He could never know what had just happened.

She took a step back and leaned against the opposite handrail, attempting a semblance of normality that she did not feel. Inside, she was a shaking, quivering wreck of nerves. "Who, me?" She feigned a laugh, "I'm fine." If recent months had taught her anything, it was to play it cool in her worst moments.

Connor did not seem too convinced. "Are you sure?" he persisted.

"Yes, of course!" She forced herself to laugh. "I must have eaten something that didn't agree with me." She smiled at him —or tried to. What she needed was to get away and be by herself, but she also knew that if she did, she would only replay *that* scene over and over in her head and torture herself all day long. That wouldn't help either.

She looked around, expecting to find Silvia sashaying past any minute, but there was no sign of her. "Where's your girlfriend?" Surprise flittered across her face as she appraised his casual attire—a loose button up with a pair of jeans. It was so far removed from the always suited Connor, the man with no time for anything or anyone but his court cases.

Gone was that on-edge and rushed look that he'd worn during the last months they had been together. Now his features were softer, less hard-edged; it reminded her of what had originally attracted her to him. In this moment, concentrating on Connor seemed to help her avoid thinking about her mistake. Nico.

"She's not my girlfriend. And I don't know or care where she is."

"Really?" The news startled Ava. "Even so, Verona agrees with you." Ava felt uncomfortable at the way he was staring at her; it was so intense, it made her feel jittery. If he stared too long, he would know something was up.

"I had an amazing girlfriend once, she became my fiancée, but I really fucked up." His eyes drifted over to her hand, as she brought it to rest by her side. A light flip in her belly was the first indication that something was wrong. Was Connor professing something for her, again?

Please, not now.

She didn't need more drama in her life. "Please stop, Connor," she begged. She had no intimate feelings for Connor, but she needed his friendship right at this very moment. She couldn't be alone. Not able to articulate what she wanted to say, because she did not know how to respond to him, she sought an easy way out. "Do you have anything planned today?"

"Nothing. I'm free. It's my last day here and I'm glad I bumped into you. I've not seen you around lately." His words had a harsh edge to them.

She ignored his implied question. She didn't want to talk about where she had been these past few days. The queasiness in her stomach reappeared and she wondered if she could carry through with the idea that had suddenly come to her.

As she stood across the steps from Connor, she thought how crazy it was that they had both ended up here, now, in this very moment. They were almost a world apart from the people they had been less than a year ago. But if they had gotten as far as the wedding, this is where they would have been, on honeymoon, as a couple.

She suddenly saw Connor as the man she had first met, not the Connor he had become. She had changed, too.

Perhaps she was not wholly blameless in all of the things that had gone wrong in their relationship. Things which she had shamelessly stuck together, like a patchwork blanket, put together from different bits and pieces but in the end looked so higgledy piggledy, that it didn't work.

She suddenly missed *that* Connor, the man she had met and loved before his work pressures got in the way. Before he had turned out to be someone completely different: the wrong man for her.

Was she always destined to find Mr. Right and end up with Mr. Wrong?

She knew what she needed to do. It was just a matter of doing it. And love and romance and all that crazy stuff had no part in it.

"You remember that time at Cancun?" He shook her back to the present. The minute he said it, she remembered, and they both laughed at the same time. This was what she needed. Anything to take her mind off Nico. "Remember the Sorgensons?" They were a couple who had stayed at the same resort and had argued the whole time. They bickered over breakfast, scolded over lunch, and had full-blown screaming matches by evening. Yet while lying on the sun loungers, they both rolled their whale-sized frames and quietly read. Their only point of contention seemed to be around mealtimes.

Ava and Connor both laughed long and hard at the remembrance of that time.

When the hotel doors suddenly flung open, she stopped laughing. The woman who had been with Nico bounced out with Nico close on her heels. His face was already dark and somber, but his features darkened even more at the sight of her and Connor. Ava turned away before their eyes met, grateful that Connor was beside her and knowing that Nico would not say anything to her in his presence.

"Yeah, that was a great holiday." Connor stopped laughing, pausing to remember that time. He hadn't even looked up to see who was coming out of the hotel.

"Yes, it was." Ava agreed and forced herself to stare directly at Connor's face. She heard Nico's voice address the woman sharply. "I hope I made myself very clear."

His tone surprised Ava, but she knew he would try anything to explain away his actions. She was not going to fall for any of it anymore.

As the woman rushed down the steps and past her, Ava speculated on the woman's dress sense, thinking how inappropriately she was dressed, in a tight pair of trousers, a tight top with a wide-open neck and the tops of her breasts spilling over.

So, *that* was how Nico liked his women.

Even after the woman had gone, Nico hesitated at the top of the stairs. Ava knew he was waiting for her to look at him, but she didn't move her head in his direction at all.

A few seconds later, he disappeared through the doors, leaving Connor staring at her with a bucket load of questions.

CHAPTER THIRTY

Nico thundered into his office and slammed the door so hard the hinges shook.

Gina peered over her shoulder and frowned. She had never seen him this angry before. Never.

Most definitely never over a woman. She snuck out from behind the reception desk and skirted over to the hotel doors, taking a discreet peek out.

She saw Ava and Connor talking and laughing. Gina sighed and nodded her head. No wonder.

She returned to her desk, all the while mulling over the transformation that she had become a witness to. Nico was changing before her very eyes. Never had she seen him at such a loss when it came to dealing with a woman.

But then again, she had never seen him so besotted by a woman, either. He was completely in love with Ava. This was new territory, and he was fighting to find his ground in it.

She got on with her task of checking the day's bookings when the door behind her opened quietly.

Nico walked up to her, his face guarded, but she could see right through his mask. She saw the way he had practically thrown the other woman out and wondered how much of his anger was as a result of her.

He pretended to be busy and flicked through the hotel guest book. But Gina knew better and could sense he wanted to talk. She moved her attention away from her computer screen and faced him.

"Your father seems to be enjoying himself, showing Mrs. Ramirez around Verona." He avoided looking at her, choosing instead to focus on the scribbles of writing in the guest book.

"It's very kind of him, don't you think?"

Nico scowled. "Yes."

Gina waited patiently for him to elaborate, but he pretended to be preoccupied. She would have to nudge him into a confession.

"How was your trip to Riccione?"

Nico folded his arms, his body stiff, his facial expression tight. "Fine."

"Fine?" she asked, putting down her pen and surveying him with interest. She changed the subject. "What did she want?"

"Her ex-fiancé, by the looks of things."

Gina tilted her head back slightly. "I meant the woman who was in your office earlier."

Nico flexed his fingers and stretched his frame taller. "She was a meddling, nosey journalist. I'm fed up with the lot of them." He banged his balled-up fist against the table, making Gina jump.

She was onto something here. "What did she want?"

"I *thought* she wanted to do a piece on the hotel. At least that's what she told me when she asked to meet me. She said she had read some great reviews online and she wanted to know what we were doing so well. She wanted to know our 'secret.'"

Gina huffed. "She looked like trouble, turning up dressed like *that*."

"But she started asking about my past, my girlfriends, the parties, the drinking, the drugs..."

Gina dipped her chin down and looked at him, disapproval etched all over her face.

"Soft drugs," he said, as if that made up for his vices. "The debauchery, the excess—"

Gina put her hand up to halt him. "I get the picture."

"She threatened to blackmail me. She knew about my trip to Riccione with Ava. She implied blackmail, said she had photos of us together and threatened to print them if I didn't give her an exclusive, a final story about my past. She said she would write about the 'new' me and leave out Ava's photos, if I gave her a good story."

"Crazy woman."

"I wish I hadn't agreed to see her. She showed me photos of us in Ravenna, taken as recently as yesterday. I can't believe these people are still following me around. Ava hates the whole publicity angle. She has problems dealing with my past as it is. The last thing I'd want is photos of her printed all over the place. Ava would hate that. She would hate *me*. She wants her privacy. She can just about deal with seeing *me* in the press. My past exploits are what make her the unhappiest ..." Nico's voice trailed off at the end.

He was changing. Gina could see that. So, what was the problem between the two of them now?

Nico continued. "She got up to leave and threw the photos at me. I couldn't bear to have any more of these parasites blackmail me. Threatening me with Ava's privacy? No way. So, I ..." His face reddened as he seemed to relive the moment.

"What did you do, Nico?" asked Gina, glad he was talking to her as a friend now. He needed her help.

"I pushed her against the wall, I was so angry—"

Gina rolled her eyes, dreading to think what followed next.

"Then I grabbed her wrists and warned her to never, ever think of blackmailing me again. I told her to get the hell out. And that I would seek out an injunction against the lot of them."

"Did you hurt her?"

"No. I swear! It wasn't my intention. I was mad. I pushed her, but not hard. I grabbed her wrists, but not hard. I don't know. Maybe I did." He shook his head, rubbing his eyebrows furiously.

"Then Ava walked in and saw us—it was only a second. I don't know. I turned and then she was gone. Maybe she got the wrong idea. I mean, she knows I wouldn't do anything like that. I don't know. I have no idea what she thought."

Gina exhaled loudly. "Nico! Didn't you explain?"

"No, I didn't. If I'd gone running after Ava, the journalist would have had her story. She'd have printed more lies. She already had pictures of us together. Can you imagine the lies she would have made up if she'd seen me running after her? I wasn't going to give her the satisfaction. And then by the time I kicked her out, Ava was busy with Connor. It didn't seem like the right time."

"*Didn't seem like the right time?*" Gina sucked in her breath, "Nico, you *need* to tell her what went on. Why are you telling *me*? You should be telling *her*." She fanned her fingers out against her breastbone. This man was so well experienced with women, and yet so dumb and stupid at the same time. She shook her head, looking at him as he stood with his head lowered. "This woman means the world to you. You need to save this." She stepped toward him feeling concerned because, for the first time, he seemed so fragile.

He lifted his head, a cold, flinty gaze hardening his expression. "By the looks of things, she's busy."

He turned around and disappeared into his office.

The moment for talking had passed. Nico retreated into his office and sank back into his chair.

With his elbows on the table and hands joined together as if in prayer, Nico rested his chin against his index fingers. He closed his eyes for a moment, letting the darkness shut out the world outside.

No matter what he did or how hard he tried, he could not convince people to change their opinions of him. His reputation preceded him and affected his life even now, many years later.

He had failed again with Ava. But after their recent time together where they had talked late into the night and he'd opened up to her in a way he never had with anyone else, could she not see the real him? Why would she think there was anything going on with the woman?

Didn't she know him better by now? Maybe he could make her see—she just needed more time to get used to this. She was trying. She'd been more understanding during their trip, especially when she'd found the magazine of him at the Grand Prix party. Maybe, in her own way, and slowly, she was finally coming to see that he wasn't a playboy anymore and that he was in love with her. He hadn't told her that, of course, because he didn't want to scare her off.

He had wanted to explain everything about that other woman, but Ava had been with Connor. Nico's jaw tightened at the idea of her with her ex-fiancé. Why was she laughing and talking with him as though they were suddenly best friends?

He'd make it up to her, but he couldn't think about that now. He had a lot to deal with today. He would catch up with her later, once he'd made a few calls regarding the hotel in Ravenna.

Hopefully by then that idiot ex of hers would have long gone.

CHAPTER THIRTY-ONE

Ava watched Nico walk back inside. She felt the urge to run after him and demand an explanation; she needed to know that what she had seen had been a huge mistake.

But her eyes had not deceived her.

Splintered memories of the days in Riccione and Ravenna pricked her consciousness. Andrea's warning replayed over and over in her ears while images of Nico's hands around the woman's arms burned in her mind.

Now she understood why Nico had told her to take it easy and rest up, why he had not wanted her to come to the hotel today. But it didn't make any sense. Why would Nico take such a huge risk with that woman? Why not be discreet?

Her logical side tried to reason it out, but her emotional side knew. She knew what she had seen and no matter how she tried to explain it all away, she had seen him and that woman up against a wall. She wished his father had walked in on him. But she might never have known the extent of Nico's deceit if she hadn't experienced it herself.

No, it was better it had happened the way it did.

She understood now why Nico had been interested in her

in the first place. It had been only because she had been unattainable. Now that he'd had her, and taken the best of her, he was already bored.

The only problem was she had fallen for him.

He had built her up to believe in love again, only to break her again. She had been delusional to even consider a future with this man. A future she would always regret because being by Nico's side meant having to fight off all the other women who would flock to him. That would never stop. It wasn't his fault that he was so good-looking and attracted these types of women with his family name and money. But if he cared for her, as he said he did, then he would know how to resist. Did he love her? That was the question. He'd never said anything about love.

Perhaps Nico was insatiable? Maybe one woman would *never* be enough?

She would never be enough.

Despite making a promise to herself that she could not, would not take on another man who could break her heart again, how was it that she had ended up in another relationship that had disaster written all over it?

Her DNA was wired to attract men who would only hurt her. That's why.

Lost deep in her thoughts, she didn't hear Connor until he waved his hand at her. "A penny for your thoughts?" He made no move to come closer and for that she was grateful.

"You're going back home tomorrow," she noted, her voice dull. It was time she also booked her flight back home.

"My quest failed. I didn't win you back. There's nothing to do but admit defeat and go home." Connor looked pensive.

"Would you like to spend the day with me, in Montova?" It would mean she wouldn't be alone to mope over Nico, nor would he approach her with any more lies and explanations.

She needed to speak to Andrea about the shipments anyway, and then she would book her flight home. She'd go home tomorrow if she could, without even waiting for her mom and Rona. They could stay here for as long as they wanted.

She was still reeling from the pain in her heart but moping around all day crying would not fix a thing. As sick and as tired as she felt, for this had totally drained her energy, she had to keep busy.

Connor looked confused. "Are you asking me to spend the day with you?"

"Unless you have something else planned."

"I'm free. I can't think of a nicer way to spend my last day here." Surprise was glued to his face.

Ava pulled out her cell phone and switched it off. She wanted no contact from Nico at all. "Let's go." She turned and went down the steps.

"Now?" He followed her anyway.

"Yes." Before she changed her mind.

She could tell by the way he spoke, without even turning around, that he had a huge smile on his face. "What's in Montova?"

"Products, for my online business."

"You're still doing your clothing site?" he asked.

"It's a baby site," she corrected him. He had never had much interest in it before.

"Yeah, sure. I remember now. You're still doing that, huh? Interesting."

Interesting?

"You were always so passionate about it."

You noticed?

"I still am. I've found some new products to sell and I'm going to have them shipped back. You don't have to come, I mean, if it sounds boring." Give him a get out clause. No need to ruin his last day in Verona just because her day had been obliterated to bits.

"No, no!" He seemed animated, like a little puppy, eager to please. "I would love to see your new products. That's exciting stuff. I had no idea you had been working so hard." This was way more than he had ever said to her about her side hobby, which was what the website had been initially.

He had never had much time for her or her projects before.

She blushed, loving the adoration, since it did not come from Connor often. "I was wrong for thinking you'd only come out here for your own selfish reasons. When really you did it to get your life back after the terrible way I treated you." His interpretation of things made her look up.

Ava shrugged her shoulders. She skipped the soul-searching; it was time to be pragmatic now. She didn't want to get entangled in any more dramas. She was only asking Connor along to keep her company, not so that he could win her back.

"We'll get a taxi," she said, looking back at the hotel. She decided not to use the hotel driver even though Nico always insisted on it. It didn't seem the right thing to do now.

Being a lovelorn emotional wreck had only resulted in more heartache.

She was done with love.

She was done with Verona, and all of Italy, too.

CHAPTER THIRTY-TWO

"Tori want to go out?" Rona knelt on the floor and buttoned up her daughter's white fleece.

The little girl nodded excitedly.

"All right then, we'll go for a walk." Rona rummaged through her rucksack, making sure she had everything she needed for a day out. She opened up the lightweight stroller, the one necessity without which she could not leave. The stroller would cramp her style, but it would have to do. It was better than carrying Tori around, something that she would *not* be able to do in her high-heeled wedges.

Tori gurgled excitedly; she already knew what this meant. The promise of outside.

"Come on then, little lady. Seems like Grandma's deserted us for another day." Tori pulled a mischievous smile. Too true, thought Rona. She had never seen this coming, her mother cavorting around Verona with a stranger.

Okay, the man wasn't a total stranger, and he and his family had been good to them, but if she had known her mother would be enjoying herself *this* much, she wouldn't have let Carlos return home so quickly. Whether his father needed him or not.

A few minutes later, Rona set out, pushing the stroller in front of her with as much aplomb as she could. She tucked her butt in and her chest out. For a new mother, she looked good, and she knew it.

Wandering around Verona pushing a stroller did not hold much appeal for Rona, but she couldn't stay cooped up inside any longer. It also grated on her that her own mother had done more sightseeing than she had. Mingling with tourists and visiting places was not Rona's thing, but wandering around the town center, looking in all the shops was manageable.

Naturally, they would have to stop for lunch at Gioberti's again. She liked the food there. Tori did, too.

Elsa stifled the growing ball of excitement that rose in her throat.

Shaking her head, she laughed out loud at another one of Edmondo's anecdotes. She hadn't laughed so much in a long time. She felt so light and cheery and surprised at herself for having such a wonderful time with him.

If anyone had told her a few weeks ago that she would be spending time with a strange man in a foreign country, she would never have believed them. But it had happened.

She wondered what her friends back home would make of it all.

Her world had become one full of surprises and she was loving every minute of it.

"What do you think of this? Beautiful, no?" asked Edmondo, pointing to the ceiling of the Basilica di San Zeno

Maggiore. Inside were beautiful, elaborately carved panels depicting biblical scenes.

Elsa found herself breathless on more than a few occasions. Often, the craftsmanship and sheer beauty of these places she visited took her breath away.

She wandered over to the side, to a table lit up with candles. Edmondo must have sensed her need to be alone, because he nodded his head gently and walked farther away.

The quiet inside the church seduced visitors into peaceful contemplation. She took a candle and lit it, closing her eyes and saying a prayer of thanks and remembering her husband. She felt happy being here with Edmondo, going around Verona, but her husband was never far from her heart or mind.

She found her way to a pew and took a seat, contemplating her sudden and unexpected friendship with this handsome elderly gentleman. Until a few weeks ago their worlds would have never collided. Now, without trying, she felt a bond, a friendship or maybe more, that she had not been looking for but had attracted into her life all the same.

She didn't feel guilty for enjoying the company of this good, kind and gentle man, a man and a friendship that she sensed her daughters did not fully approve of. She closed her eyes, losing herself in the void, the absence of noise, reveling in the peace and solitude that gave her thoughts clarity. What she and Edmondo had was purely platonic and there was no way that either of them were hankering for anything more. Was there? They were simply two single people who enjoyed one another's company.

Keeping her head bowed and her eyes closed, an image of her beloved appeared in her thoughts and just as suddenly it vanished. It had been hard in the beginning, to deal with the grief. There had been many years when all she could do just to get through the day was to put one foot in front of the other and keep going. Because her girls had needed her, she had had no option but to do just that. In a way, they had been her salvation. Then one day, she had woken up and accepted that she was truly alone. By then, a good many years had gone by, and her daughters no longer needed her as much.

Reaching the acceptance of her husband's death had been a turning point for Elsa.

It had allowed her to cope with the thought that she would never see him again. She could at last sit at her table and eat her dinner, alone, without imagining the conversation they might have had. Accepting his passing had given her the freedom to move forward in her life.

But now she had suddenly been thrust into Edmondo's world, a man who was almost like her counterpart, in that he, too, was a widower and alone. He, too, wanted only to enjoy the rest of his days.

Was it so bad that they had met?

As if in answer, she felt a gentle touch on her shoulder. Still clasping her hands together, she lifted her head and opened her eyes.

Soft, warm eyes gazed down at her, and Edmondo smiled. There was nothing forward or inappropriate in his touch. He wanted to know if she was all right. In answer, she smiled back and shifted along the pew, making room for him. He gave her a grateful movement of his head and sat down.

They sat together for a long while, enjoying the quiet.

Rona rammed the stroller onto the pavement. Did these people not have any children?

After hours of walking around everywhere and buying a

few toys and clothes for Tori, Rona walked up to her favorite place in the whole of Verona. Gioberti's.

The owner, Gioberti, leapt toward Rona as soon as he set eyes on her. She immediately straightened her body up as she pushed the stroller into the restaurant. Tori gurgled happily in the seat with her little soft doll still in her hands.

"Bella! So nice to see you again." Gioberti flashed a blinding white smile at Rona who reciprocated eagerly. She liked the way he scanned her appearance from top to bottom.

Gioberti was always at his best when taking care of his patrons, especially if they were of the female persuasion.

"Is this good for you?" He waved his arm at a table just inside and to the corner. Rona nodded her agreement and Gioberti rattled off orders to his staff in blinding fast Italian.

Within seconds, a highchair appeared from thin air, closely followed by a menu, two wine glasses and a coloring book and crayons for Tori.

Rona sat down, relishing the attention that was being heaped upon her and which she readily lapped up.

Tori was content with her coloring project, even though she was much too young to know what to do with crayons. Rona kept a close watch on her each time she tried to put a crayon into her mouth.

In the distance Elsa and Edmondo walked along the street, not quite arm in arm but with a closeness about them.

"Isn't that...your granddaughter?" Edmondo pointed a few yards away, to the front of Gioberti's. Elsa squinted and looked. It most certainly was. Rona with Tori. "Shall we go there?"

"Is the food nice?" Elsa asked.

"It's average, though there are better places. I don't think your daughter looks happy."

Elsa looked over. Edmondo was right. Rona's mouth was clamped together tightly. Nothing resembling a smile was about to come from those lips anytime soon. Surprised at herself for even considering going to a restaurant that served better food, even though her daughter sat miserably in front of her, Elsa moved in the direction of Gioberti's. "Let's find out whether she wants us to join her."

Tori shrieked with delight as Grandma's familiar face moved closer and kissed her on the cheeks. She held her arms out in an expectant hug and sent her crayons rolling to the ground.

"My little Tori!" Elsa bent over to lift her granddaughter out of the highchair.

"Don't get her out, Mom! I'm trying to settle her down to eat." Rona looked grumpy.

Elsa let go of her granddaughter, leaving her to wail in the chair. "Do you mind if we join you?" she asked, examining Rona's face for clues. She cast her gaze briefly over Rona's plate, which was still full of uneaten salad.

Rona replied, "Go ahead." Elsa watched her daughter's face, trying to gauge the real cause of her mood. She sensed that her daughter didn't approve much of her wandering around Verona with Edmondo.

"Hey, Mr. Cazale," said Rona, acknowledging him.

"Are you sure you don't mind?" he asked carefully, as he pulled out a chair for Elsa. Elsa sat down, knowing that her daughter really seemed in need of company. Rona shook her head.

"No, Mr. Cazale. Please, join us. Mom has made herself more than comfortable here."

Edmondo complied happily and the four of them sat

together. Over in the background, Gioberti was busy talking to two tall and lithe students who had walked in moments before. Rona could see them from the corners of her eyes.

"You eat," said Elsa, taking Tori's bowl from Rona. "I'll finish feeding her." Rona looked as miserable as hell. Food might cheer her up a little. Elsa knew she had not been sleeping well.

CHAPTER THIRTY-THREE

The taxi sped along the road and fields of lush green grass, as thick and silky as chenille, scooted past them.

Ava stared out, lost in thought. Going to Montova with Connor? Was she insane?

Her world of late had teetered from mixed emotions about her past, and sheer bliss about her future.

Until this morning.

What future?

"Amazing scenery," Connor commented, looking out of the window.

That future?

What was she doing? She could have confronted Nico and demanded an explanation. Even if it was just for pure entertainment. She would have liked to see him talk himself out of *that one.*

With relish, she remembered the look of anguish in his eyes when he had come across her with Connor on the stairs. She had deliberately looked away when he tried to catch her eye. But that didn't stop her feeling his eyes burning into her.

It was so obvious that he had wanted to talk. But she would never give him the satisfaction of explaining himself.

Instead of hearing his explanation, or lies, she had leapt in the opposite direction and done something equally stupid. So here she was in a taxi with Connor, on the way to Montova.

She'd thought having Connor with her would help her lose herself in the numbness. Nico had ripped out her heart. Connor was her distraction, much like a clown in a circus.

She should have felt bad for using him that way. But she considered it payback. And she was in no mood to be nice today.

He was spurting on about something, but her mind was subdued. She was hanging onto a semblance of normality by the wisp of a thread. The slightest tremor in her world now would send her hurtling down that dark crevice she had been in when she had arrived here.

Connor was asking her if there were any nice restaurants in Montova. *He'll want to share a meal together,* thought Ava with a touch of dismay. She would have to make it clear that they would go to Montova and back and nothing else.

The whole point of going to Montova was so that she could check with Andrea about the shipment of all the products she had ordered. She wasn't sure if Nico had taken care of them, as he had intended to. So much had happened between them lately. And she didn't want to ask him. She also needed to do a final check of her inventory. She'd been putting it off forever. At times she wondered if she was really ready to leave.

Now that time had come.

There was no way in hell she would accept Nico's help anymore. She would have to work quickly and not let Connor drag things along, slowing her down. Now that she was removed from the Casa Adriana and Nico, she regretted her decision to bring Connor with her.

What she really wanted right at this moment was to return to the pensione and lie down. She felt more drained than ever, and it wasn't even noon yet.

Connor boldly rested his hand over hers, lightly brushing against her thighs on which her hand rested. "I'm sorry. I'm jabbering on like an idiot." He laughed, a short little chuckle. This was not the Connor that she knew at all. Connor did not talk this much, let alone worry about her feelings, or seek out her opinions, and least of all chuckle much.

Had the air in Verona changed him, too? It seemed to be having an effect on everyone else around her.

"This must have been a lucky find for you." He waved vaguely at the outdoors.

"Nico brought me here. He was keen for me to find new products."

"He was, huh?"

The taxi pulled to a slow stop as they arrived in Montova. Ava got out and wondered exactly what she was getting herself out of, and what she was throwing herself into.

They had been in Andrea's warehouse no longer than half an hour and already the pride Ava had felt in her new products had ebbed away.

Total insanity had possessed her to allow Connor a glimpse into this new life of hers.

Andrea had stored all of Ava's products in one corner of the huge warehouse and Ava walked around, checking it all against her inventory. The items she had ordered from

Natale's clothing factory had been sent here, too, keeping everything together in one place.

Ava jerked her head up sharply at another one of Connor's pointless interruptions.

"I'm not so sure." He pulled a distasteful face and ran his hand slowly across his cheek, all the while staring at a pile of items neatly stacked along the shelves.

Ava decided to let him have his moment before she had hers. She took a step closer to see what he was going on about. It was a beautifully carved wooden clock face with a string attached to the bottom that, when pulled, emitted a tune from a well-known lullaby.

"What are you not so sure about?"

"I mean..." He toyed with the clock in one hand and pulled the string with the other. Instantly the tune started, a little tinny, but soothing all the same. The clock was beautifully made; it was the kind of toy that was hard to find in the big toy and department stores back home. Ava had fallen in love with it the very first time she'd set eyes on it.

She reached out to pluck it from Connor's hand, but he managed to dodge her easily. In one swift movement he held it beyond her grasp.

"Come on, Ava." He pulled the cord again and setting off the tune once more. "Do you really think children used to bright lights and electronic tunes are going to be interested in this?" He held it up with disdain.

"Their parents will be."

"These might not do as well as you think." There he went again, stamping his negative opinion on everything. "I'm sorry, Ava, but I thought you wanted an honest opinion." He handed the clock back to her, then sheepishly looked around at the other merchandise. Spotting a baby crib, he crawled over to examine it in more detail. "Now this, this looks good.

Very authentic." He ran his hands over the dark finished wood. "How are you shipping these over?"

She took a wild guess. "In containers."

"Flat packed?"

"Yes."

"Do you have the necessary insurance in place?"

"Of course. Don't worry, none of this is your problem." She forced a confident smile at Connor. Nico would have taken care of all of this. Now she had a bigger headache to contend with, not being familiar with the Italian rules and regulations. Time was running out. She wanted to go home the first flight she could get.

"But does this wood conform to our fire safety regulations?"

The thought hadn't even occurred to her. With a slowly deflating spirit, Ava wished she hadn't brought Connor here. He had soiled all her brightest dreams with his dour attitude, even if he was right.

She hadn't thought things through. She'd known about fire and safety regulations, but she hadn't checked them out. This was often her failing, jumping into things feet first and worrying about the consequences later. She was the dreamer, while Connor was the realist.

His personality had always dampened her fire. Was this the basis of their fundamental differences? The thing that had slowly, over time, led to a break in their relationship?

"Sorry about that, Ava." Andrea appeared suddenly. She had been dealing with a group of buyers for most of the time they had been here.

After a brief introduction to Connor, they all stood around looking at the large pile of products that now belonged to Ava. Ava sucked in her breath sharply and prayed that Connor would not carry on with his withering comments.

"Piled together like this, it really looks a lot." Andrea swept her arm from one end of the neatly piled boxes to the other.

Ava became alarmed and tried hard not to give in to the flood of emotions which swirled around her. She might have gotten a little carried away when she'd been ordering stock. The pile was huge now that everything was all heaped together. But she had checked her figures twice, and though she had spent a lot, it wasn't as much as the pile made it look. Andrea had given her good prices. It was the shipping costs she was dreading.

Ava left Connor to his own devices and prayed he would remain interested enough in the products to stay out of her hair for a while.

"I must get on," she explained to Andrea as she walked toward the opposite side of the store, away from Connor. Andrea followed her and Ava resumed checking things off on her inventory.

Andrea nodded her head towards Connor. "He doesn't seem as bad as you described him."

"Something about the air in Verona," Ava said wearily. "It seems to be having a peculiar effect on most people who come here."

"Do you know how much it will cost to have this shipped back?" Andrea peered over Ava's shoulder at her calculations.

"Nico was going to take care of it for me. Didn't he get in touch with you about it?" She knew he had her Denver address. "Apparently he has contacts who can secure me a good deal."

Andrea shook her head. "He hasn't mentioned it. But you don't have to worry if Nico's taking care of it. You're in good hands."

No, I'm not. You were right all along.

More customers arrived and Andrea headed toward them before Ava stopped her. She pulled her arm gently. "Andrea," Ava started to say something, but the mere mention of Nico had caused tears to well up in her eyes. What was wrong with her? She thought she had recovered from that episode this morning.

"Ava?" Concern shadowed Andrea's face. She turned her back on the new customers and stared at her friend. "You don't look so well. What's wrong?"

"Nothing." Ava struggled to keep her voice level. "I'm going back to Denver, the first flight out—"

"So soon? What about your family?"

"I should have gone home a long time ago." She fought to hold it all together. "Andrea, I need you to do something for me, please. I will pay you but I don't think I can stay here a moment longer."

Andrea stood solemnly by her side, refusing to budge. "Just say it."

"Nico's very busy at the hotel. Could you deal with my shipping instead of him? You must have people that you use, or maybe your cousin has contacts?"

Andrea shook her head. "We don't export."

Ava's face fell.

"But if Nico's dealing with this then—"

"No." Ava's voice took on a pleading tone. "I'd rather you took care of it, not Nico."

Andrea narrowed her eyes. "Is something going on between the two of you? I knew there was a spark, I suspected as much. Tell me, are you —"

Ava shook her head before Andrea could finish. "It was a mistake. I should have taken your word for it. I should never have gotten involved." She sniffled and managed to keep the tears at bay.

"What's happened? Why are you upset? Nico's a good man, underneath it all. He's had a lot to deal with over the years."

"You warned me. I should have listened to you. He can't be trusted." She fought back the sobs.

"But he's a changed man, now. He thinks the—"

Ava sniffled, shaking her head. "Andrea, stop. I don't want to hear it. No more about Nico." And then before she could stop herself, the tears started falling, faster than she could stop them.

Alarmed by Ava's sudden breakdown in front of her, Andrea put her arms around her friend and comforted her. "Hey, hey, now then. It can't be that bad." She handed a Kleenex to Ava, who blew like a foghorn into it. Andrea hushed. "Don't you worry another minute about the shipping. Leave it to me."

"Thank you. You've got all my details, haven't you?" Ava asked, between sobs. She turned her face sideways, as she caught Connor looking over. He was the last person she wanted finding out about her whole sorry fiasco.

Andrea nodded, then touched Ava's arm. "Don't you worry about a thing."

"Thanks, Andrea. I'm so sorry. I thought I had more time. I thought Nico, I—" The tears welled up again as she remembered the time when she had first met Andrea. When Nico had introduced them both. He had known that Montova would be a great place for Ava to find products. He had always wanted the best for her.

Which was why his actions this morning completely confused her. She didn't know what to believe anymore. She just wanted to go home.

Andrea's arms went around her again. "I don't know what

happened between you two. I don't understand, but you really should talk to him."

Ava shook her head harder. "No," she said sharply. "I've seen enough. I don't want to talk about it." Afraid that if she started crying again, she would not stop, she begged Andrea. "Please, I can't let him see me like this." She nodded in Connor's direction.

"When are you leaving?" Andrea asked.

"On the first flight out that I can get."

"You take care of yourself, and we'll keep in touch. Promise me?"

"I promise."

The women hugged each other tightly before Andrea left her and tended to her new customers.

Connor waved a wooden drum set at her. "I can see these selling like hotcakes," he said enthusiastically, before he realized that something was wrong. He rushed towards Ava.

"What's wrong? You don't have to hide it from me. I can tell when you've been crying. Is it him again?" He had never been so perceptive before.

"No," she lied. "It's hay fever."

"You've never had hay fever in your life. Come on, Ava. I might have been out of your life for a while now, but I still know you well enough."

Desperate to get some fresh air and to get away, she steeled herself and turned away.

"Let's go," she said, not even turning around to see if he had heard her or not. She'd asked the cab driver to return after noon and he should have already been here. Seeing no sign of the taxi outside sent Ava's mood spiraling again. All she wanted to do was to go to bed.

"Are we heading back already? Let's grab a bite to eat first." Connor's suggestion went down like a lead balloon.

She thought of heading over to Montagnano.
Nico's village.
No. She could never go back there again, ever.
She glanced around her at Montova.
No more coming back here either.

CHAPTER THIRTY-FOUR

While waiting for the taxi, they bought two panini from a nearby sandwich shop even though Ava wasn't feeling particularly hungry. Her stomach was still queasy from the morning.

These panini were nothing like the ones made by Ermete at the village Nico had taken her to.

Every thought in her head seemed tied to Nico. He was going to be hard to forget but she needed to get him out of her system super-fast. She willed the taxi to come, just so that she could book her flights, pack, and keep her fingers crossed that she would be home by this time next week at the latest.

Connor, who knew no better, having never tasted Ermete's offerings, was in heaven. The juices from the olive oil infused vegetables dripped out of his panino and trickled down his chin.

"Nico showed you this place, you say?" Connor was on the prowl for more information.

"Yes."

"I don't recall seeing this in any of the guides I've read."

"I don't think it's a touristy place. It's a wholesale village. The locals all know about it."

"The advantages of dating the locals."

She glared at him.

"How much do you actually know about this man?" asked Connor.

Probably more than I knew about you when I first started dating you.

"Enough." Ava was beginning to feel uncomfortable with his line of questioning. He was a lawyer after all, and she wasn't sure where he was taking this. He'd seen her upset and he was fishing for news.

"Nico grew up around here; his village is a little further on."

Connor took another huge mouthful and half-snorted. "No wonder."

"No wonder what?"

"No wonder he's trying to better himself. Shake off his hillbilly roots and pass himself off as some high-flying businessman." There was no holding him back now.

"Are you feeling threatened?"

He scoffed. "I'm merely speculating. You can take the man out of the village but you can't take the village out of the man." A thinly sliced mushroom balanced precariously on his bottom lip.

She could tell that he hated Nico. But more than anger for the man who had captured her heart fleetingly, in Connor Ava saw contempt as well.

"If you're suggesting he's ashamed of his roots, you're wrong. Nico loves his roots. He's not ashamed of who he is." She was talking as though she knew the real Nico and now she wasn't so sure anymore. Up until this morning she might have thought she had an insight into him. But since then, everything she thought she knew about him had vanished.

She had no idea why she was defending him.

"I don't understand what you see in him anyway," Connor retorted, and silenced Ava at once. "I don't want to see you upset again, Ava. This, me badmouthing Nico"—he flailed his hands towards his chest—"it's wrong. I hardly know the man. The only thing I have against him is that he has *you*." He rested his hands on his lap and looked at her with the most honest expression, stripped bare of the arrogant, know-it-all Connor. "I fucked up. I fucked up when I let you go. And I fucked up when I tried to get you back. But when I saw you had eyes for no one but that man, I couldn't get in the way and mess things up for you again. So, I tried to make you jealous." He shook his head.

"Silvia? Was that it?"

He hung his head in shame. "It was a pitiful attempt."

Ava nodded in agreement, half-humbled by his last-minute attempt at coming clean.

"Look, Ava. I walked away because you looked so happy. In Venice..." His voice trailed off, and she wondered if he had remembered the scene when he had walked in on them.

"It's fine, you don't need to—"

"Let me finish, please. I'm going home tomorrow and I'm so happy you gave me this chance to spend the day with you."

She felt suddenly ashamed for the reason *why* she chose to spend time with him.

"You looked happier than I'd seen you in ages and I knew I had failed. It's time for me to step aside, not that my attempt at winning you back ever had a chance to get off the ground in the first place."

The candid look in his eyes softened her heart. More than anything, Connor's plea seemed sincere. She warmed at his words, and though she didn't feel anything like happy today, she managed a half smile.

"I can tell that you're upset about something. Ever since I saw you this morning, I could tell something was up. But it's okay. You don't have to say anything, not if you don't want to."

She was glad he had no clue that Nico was the cause of her heartache. Better to keep it that way.

"I'm sorry for the hurt I caused you and I hope Nico treats you better than I ever did. I hope he realizes what he's got in you."

Ava grimaced at his words. *Oh, Connor. You have no idea.* But her problem was not Connor's problem, and he need never know. Nobody ever needed to know what had happened.

She would think of an appropriate story for her mom and Rona. But that could wait. "Would you do something for me?" she asked. It was a spur of the moment decision, but the moment she made it, she knew it was the right thing to do.

"Anything."

She could trust him, now. There was nobody else she could get to do this for her. She fumbled around in her bag for the Flamentagostini bracelet, still in its box. She had worn it in Riccione and Ravenna, the whole time, and it had meant something completely different then. A token of love, of honest, pure love.

Now it was tainted.

She gave the box to Connor. "I need you to do this one thing for me, Connor. I'm trusting you, and I don't want you to ask me or anyone else any questions. Promise me?"

He was taken aback by the seriousness of her words.

"I'm worried about you," he said, taking the box from her.

"Don't be. I'm fine. I'll feel even better if you hand this

back. To Nico. Only him, or Gina if he's not around. Can you do that for me, please?"

"Of course."

"No questions asked."

"No questions asked, I promise." True to his word, even though he must have had a million things he wanted to say, Connor took the box from her gallantly and didn't ask a single question the rest of the way home.

Ava knew two things for certain.

Nico had taken her heart, but it no longer belonged to him. And Connor, the man who had broken her heart before, now became a man she could trust again.

CHAPTER THIRTY-FIVE

Tori lay asleep in the travel cot.

"Don't fuss over her, Mom," ordered Rona, waving a big curly hairbrush through her thick head of hair. Elsa stepped away quietly from the cot, unease grumbling in her belly as she watched her daughter get ready. Big hair, big earrings, and high heels.

But where was she going and with whom?

Elsa had been drafted in to look after Tori, something that Elsa looked forward to. In fact, she had turned down Edmondo's invitation to dinner so that she could be here for her daughter instead. It hadn't been a tough decision; her daughters always came first, but Elsa had felt a pang of regret that her days here were soon coming to an end.

Edmondo's face had reddened when he asked her and she had hated turning him down, but she had no other choice. Ava hadn't been around, nor had she answered her cell when Elsa had tried to get hold of her.

Elsa had been half-tempted to ask Edmondo to come over and help her babysit. She would have happily cooked for him at the pensione. After all, he had spoken of his love for grandchildren and she knew that helping her pass the time babysitting might have been something he would have enjoyed. Maybe not yet. Maybe it was early days.

Early days? What was she thinking?

"Aren't you tired?" Elsa knew her daughter had taken Tori around Verona in the morning and the meal at Gioberti's had ended up taking most of the afternoon.

"No, Mom." Rona pulled the brush through her hair, which only made it bounce bigger. "Tori should sleep through. You'll have an easy few hours."

"We have to pack." As if that would convince Rona to stay.

"We have more than a week left, Mom. Why the rush?"

"Where did you say you were going again?" Elsa didn't that Carlos had gone back to Denver so quickly and that her daughter now had a new lust for life acting out her single days again.

"I didn't."

"Do you want me to stay and babysit Tori?" threatened Elsa. She didn't like the way her daughter was behaving.

"Sorry, Mom. Why so many questions? How come you don't bug Ava as much? I thought we were here to keep an eye on her."

"I didn't think we needed to keep an eye on you, too," Elsa replied curtly. But mention of Ava had her troubled again. She would go over and see her later on. She faced Rona. "In the entire time we've been here, I've only seen you and Ava spend a couple of days together. What's going on with the two of you?" Elsa sat down at the dining table and picked up a local guide to Verona. She flicked through it dejectedly. She had been to many of these places, thanks to Edmondo, but there were still many places she wanted to visit.

They still had time, but it would end soon enough. Would she ever return?

"Ava's been too wrapped up in her playboy, or hadn't you noticed?" Rona flung the hairbrush back into her handbag and pulled out a lipstick. "Speaking of which, we hardly see you around much either. You've been quite busy yourself, huh, Mom?" Without giving Elsa a chance to reply, Rona added, "Do you think it's right for you to be gallivanting around Verona with...that...that man?"

Elsa threw the brochure down. Looking after her granddaughter was one thing but sitting here having her daughter throw such accusations at her was something else. How dare she? "His name, in case it slipped your mind, is Edmondo. He was kind enough to show me around Verona. It really is none of your business, Rona."

"What next, Mom? Are you going to start *seeing* this man? Don't you think you're past that now?" She twisted her lipstick and the magenta stick shot back down into its case. She slammed the top down and threw it back into her handbag.

Elsa stared at her feisty daughter who stood with hands on hips and nostrils flared. This new friendship of hers had definitely ruffled her daughters. She would have understood it had they been children or even teenagers going through a troubling phase. But grown women? Their response both saddened and surprised her.

"I'm not cheating on anyone, Rona. If anyone needs to be careful around here, it's you." Her words soon slapped the pout off her daughter's face.

Elsa picked the brochure back up again, but her mind was on Edmondo. She hadn't considered where her friendship might end up. It was true enough that the two of them had spent wonderful days together. Edmondo seemed just as surprised as she was by how easily they got on.

It was effortless; they both had similar stories, although she had lost her husband much earlier than he had lost his wife. Neither of them had talked about "their friendship" but they both enjoyed their time together.

Which was why it partly amused and annoyed her that her daughters had taken their companionship so seriously.

"What I do with Edmondo is up to me and not for you to worry about."

Rona stopped preening her hair in front of the mirror and glared at her mother.

Elsa slipped past her daughter to grab the one thing that would give her a little comfort. A cup of tea.

Asking Edmondo to come over for dinner was no longer an option. She decided to check in on Ava later.

According to Edmondo, Nico would be away in Rome for a few days. She guessed her daughter would be home alone. She looked forward to spending some time with her for a change. It had been a while.

As she filled up the electric kettle, Elsa's blood slowly simmered away. She shouted over her shoulder, "Maybe you should ask yourself why you're going out again today, dressed up like that when your husband is slaving away at work back at home?"

Tori stirred in her cot. Elsa quickly moved to her and bent over, laying a soothing hand over the little girl's forehead. "Don't worry about your mother," she whispered, glancing at Rona who had started angling towards the cot. In a lighter voice she added, "We'll be fine. You go, enjoy yourself, wherever you're going." Elsa's temper never remained for too long, not when it came to her children.

"Thanks, Mom." Her daughter kissed her on the cheek

and left, leaving a very perplexed Elsa standing over the travel cot.

As soon as the door closed, Tori stirred a little more, then started crying. It was as though she had a built-in tracking device straight to her mother and knew when her mother was more than a few meters away.

Elsa bent over and lifted the little girl out. She rocked her in her arms, but the crying persisted. Then Elsa sang to her, hummed at her and hugged her. But she could not do the one thing that Tori wanted—give her a mother's hug.

Over the noise of the commotion, Elsa knew her quiet evening with a nice book and a cup of tea had evaporated.

She caught sight of the stroller in the corner and knew what she would do. Even though Ava was only next-door, a small ride in the stroller would soon have her granddaughter sound asleep.

CHAPTER THIRTY-SIX

Ava lay in bed, in shock. At some point she would get up and pack. And make it over to see her mom and Rona and break the news to them.

The news about her return. Not the other news.

She wasn't sure how she was going to handle *that* news. She was having problems coming to terms with it herself.

It was almost evening and after leaving Connor at the hotel she had returned to her pensione and done nothing but lie in bed for hours.

She had done nothing, apart from *that* one thing. That one thing three times. She sat up and stared at the test stick for what seemed like the fiftieth time that evening. She had tried three tests and they all reported the same thing: Pregnant 3+.

Their baby had been conceived in Venice.

Ava slid back down on the bed and curled up. She had not seen this coming at all. Running away from Denver to get space and clarity in her life had landed her in a bigger mess than ever. In the blink of an eye, her life had become even more complicated, and it was all her fault.

She slowly ran her hand over her flat stomach and tried to imagine another life inside. But beyond her tiredness, the missed period and her recent queasiness, there was nothing to make her believe she was carrying anything other than a lot of heartache.

Nico had no idea, nor would he ever, that he was the father.

She had become slack taking her birth control pills, after all, when she came here she'd never intended to fall in love, let alone end up in anyone's bed. Even though Nico had been careful most of the time, there were a few occasions where he had forgotten protection. Despite their haphazard prevention plans, the idea that she could still end up pregnant was something that had taken her completely by shock.

Rona would never let her forget this when she found out. Ava dared not even think what her mother might have to say about it all.

A quick knock at the door ruptured her thoughts. She panicked. Nico? If she stayed quiet, he might think no one was in.

She scampered off the bed, taking all evidence of the pregnancy tests with her into the bathroom. Quickly, she discarded them in the bin and stopped as another thought grabbed her. What if he looked through her bin?

Her heart rate shot up further

Another knock on the door sent her into full-blown panic mode and she grabbed the small, plastic bin and hid it in the cupboard under the sink. Then she washed her hands.

A quick succession of knocks triggered anger and set her pulse racing. There was nothing to do now but face him. Open the door, not let him through. Tell him to leave.

She walked toward the door, pressing her hand against her chest, thinking it might silence the thumping of her heartbeat. She wished she had gone to see her mother. Surrounding herself with other people, as she had today with Connor, meant safety from Nico.

When she opened the door, her heart sank with relief. *Or was it disappointment?* "Mom?"

"What took you so long?" Her mother shuffled inside with the stroller, putting her fingers to her lips to keep the noise down. Tori had fallen asleep on the way.

"Put her here." Ava whispered. She moved the stroller to a corner of the room and wrapped the blanket snugly around the peacefully sleeping child. This way Tori was close enough to keep an eye on and yet out of direct conversation.

With the baby taken care of, Ava flung her arms around her mom holding on for dear life. "Oh, Mom! I am so happy to see you." Her words were barely audible as she muffled them into her mother's shoulder.

Elsa hugged her daughter back tightly. "What is it?" She held Ava at arm's length and looked at her carefully.

Ava shrugged off her mom's concern and walked over to the sofa where she sat down.

"Nothing, Mom. I'm...I'm..." She paused, just enough to steady her nerves. "I'm ready to go home now. I've booked my flight. I'm leaving tomorrow morning."

Her mother let out a gasp. "You're what?" Her mother could read her like a book. She had to be careful she didn't give anything away.

"Kim needs me. I need to get back."

"Kim?"

"My VA."

"I know who she is. You're going back because your virtual assistant needs you? You can run your business from here, you've been doing that for well over a month. Tell me, Ava, what are you *really* running away from?"

"Who says I'm running?"

"I do. I'm your mother."

Ava looked down at her feet, wondering how long before she would not be able to see them. A bump, a big bump. Her feet were the least of her problems.

Her mother wasn't giving up easily. "It must be serious. You've only just come back from your trip. What happened since you got back? I don't understand. And why would you book your return flight without waiting for me or Rona? Are you going to tell me?"

How could she tell her mother? *What* would she tell her?

"Have you two had a fight?"

Worse, Mom. Much worse.

"Is this about Nico having to go to Rome?"

"Rome?" she asked, puzzled, giving away the clue that she didn't know anything about Rome.

What was Nico doing in Rome? He hadn't mentioned anything about it, but then why would he? They had barely talked today.

"See if you can book me a flight out, too."

"There aren't any more available seats, Mom. I was lucky to get mine."

"Can't you wait a few days? We can all leave together."

Putting on a cheery face, Ava replied, "No, Mom. You two come when you're ready. I have to go. I know you don't believe me, but my shipments are due over there and I need to prepare."

Elsa cast a dubious glance at her daughter. "Prepare for what?"

CHAPTER THIRTY-SEVEN

"He's not here, and he won't be back for a few days unfortunately." Gina glanced at her screen, looking at Nico's calendar. She looked up at Connor and smiled. "Can I help you?"

"Please could you make sure he gets this?" Connor handed over the box Ava had given him.

Gina's eyes widened as she took the box gingerly in her hands. "This is for Nico?" she questioned. It didn't make sense.

"Yes, please make sure he gets it. Please."

"Of course. Any message?"

Connor shook his head. "No message."

Gina's brows pushed together. She had no idea why a man like Connor would be leaving anything behind for Nico. The two did not see eye to eye. Since he was checking out this morning, she put it down to some sort of unfinished business between them.

But then again, the only thing they had in common was Ava.

"Of course, sir. Did you have a pleasant stay?"

"I'm not sure."

Gina gave him a curious smile, unsure if he was being serious or joking. "Have a pleasant journey back, sir."

"Goodbye." Connor Beachcroft dipped his head by way of acknowledgement and left the hotel where he should have spent his honeymoon.

It was midday and Nico had already done a full day's work at his desk in one of the moderately well kitted out rooms of the Cazale Roma, where he was now staying.

After his arrival in Rome late yesterday evening, he had been plunged headfirst into dealing with the staff issues at the hotel.

It wasn't just the issues with the head chef and a few members of staff that were causing him concern. After a brief look around the hotel, he had examined the books as well as the rooms and processes in place, and he saw a lot of things that made him worry. This was more than a few days' work. Easily.

He had worked all through the night, until the early hours of the morning, documenting everything that needed to be done. Perhaps the first rollout should have been here and not at the Cazale Riccione. The Rome hotel always tended to be the last one to be looked at, being the farthest away. But clearly this had now brought up all sorts of problems.

And he should have started rolling out his processes a lot sooner, instead of just a few days ago. That had been the original plan. Until Ava Ramirez had shown up and thrown his life into disarray. A disarray that he had loved.

He scowled, checking his mobile for new texts or missed calls from Ava. It was pointless to do this really, because he would have heard them come in, but he checked anyway, in case he had been so busy working that he had missed them.

But there was nothing. He'd called her yesterday, after he had calmed down a little, but it only went to voicemail. He'd left a couple messages too. But she hadn't bothered to get back to him. Why was *she* so mad? If anything, *he* was the one who was hurting. The episode with the journalist and then after, seeing Ava with Connor, had left him inflamed.

He stretched his back out in the chair and placed a large palm on the back of his neck, flexing his shoulders at the same time. He had been sitting in this position for hours and his body now ached. He had more meetings with the hotel manager this afternoon and had tasked him with finding a new replacement chef.

This wasn't going to be easy and Nico wanted to have a hand in the recruitment process. He was going to be here in Rome for a few days yet.

He also had the Ravenna hotel details to work through. With so much on his plate, he promised himself to resolve the situation with Ava once he returned. Clearly, they needed to talk.

He understood now that she'd been more than upset by that incident with the journalist. But had she not realized how upset he had been to see her talking to Connor? And then she had deliberately avoided looking at him. Why had it become tit-for-tat suddenly? He hated games.

Nico ran his hands through his hair and settled back, ruminating over the events of yesterday. When his cell went off, he leapt to get it.

Disappointment smacked him when it wasn't Ava.

"What's going on, Nico?" It was his father.

"We're recruiting for a new chef today—" Nico started.

"I mean about Ava? Elsa is most upset."

Nico shot upright. "Ava? What do you mean?"

His father reported that she left for Denver this morning, according to her mother but that Elsa was no better off knowing why. He was trying to find out on her behalf.

Nico got up and paced the room frantically. Maybe he should have kept on calling her, instead of punishing her for his jealousy by playing it cool. He scratched his forehead and tried to think.

"I don't know anything, Papa. I didn't know she *had* left." Anxiety scratched his insides and he was suddenly left feeling helpless.

Now he really had to wonder. Had she been *that* angry with him that her only recourse had been to jump on the next flight home? Or was there more to it?

"Let me make a few calls, Papa, and I'll let you know."

Nico hung up and dialed Gina immediately on her cell. He looked at his watch. The flight from Verona would be landing here in Rome around now. He slipped on his jacket, getting ready to rush to the airport. He had to find out, apologize, fix it and talk some sense into her. Anything.

Gina answered and if she was surprised at him calling her directly and not on the hotel number, she didn't show it.

"Mr. Cazale, I needed to talk to—"

He cut her off. "Gina, where's Ava?"

"At the pensione." She sounded puzzled at his question, before quickly adding, "But Connor Beachcroft left a package for you this morning before he checked out."

"He's gone?"

"He flew out this morning, Denver via Rome, I believe."

Nico's heart missed a beat. "What's in the package?" he asked, though he had an inkling.

"Do you want me to open it?"

"Yes." His heart pounded fiercely against his ribcage

while he clasped the cell to his ear, wondering what to do next.

Gina gasped. "It's beautiful!"

It was the Flamentagostini bracelet. He was sure of it.

"Oh, Mr. Cazale. It's the—"

"That's all, Gina." He was brusque and rude and ended the call, before falling back into his chair.

There was no need to rush to the airport. He knew all he needed to know—why Ava had flown back, why she had returned the bracelet, and why Connor had been the one to hand it back.

She was sending him a sure sign, and she was too much of a coward to tell him to his face.

This was nothing to do with her misreading the scene with the journalist. For reasons he could not fathom, the woman he loved had decided to go back to Connor. She had chosen him over Nico.

Well, good luck to her.

Thank you for reading HONEYMOON FOR THREE! I hope you enjoyed reading more about Nico and Ava. Their story continues in HONEYMOON BLUES when Ava rushes back to Denver and wishes she had never set eyes on Nico.

Jilted once. Heartbroken twice …

Ava's insecurities make her leave Italy and return home to Denver, but a shocking turn of events reels her back to Italy. Although time will tell if she goes back into Nico's arms.

HONEYMOON BLUES is available everywhere

SIGN UP FOR MY NEWSLETTER to find out when new books release!
http://www.lilyzante.com/news

I appreciate your help in spreading the word, including telling a friend, and I would be grateful if you could leave a review on your favorite book site.

You can read an excerpt from HONEYMOON BLUE below.

Thank you and happy reading!
Lily

In Denver...

"Yes," replied Ava. She held her cell in one hand, a damp cloth in the other, and her eyes were glued to her laptop screen, now littered with images of Nico Cazale.

Multi-tasking, she was in the middle of wiping down her mom's kitchen and looking through her online store stats and emails.

But in between these two tasks, she'd ended up doing what she had been doing every time she powered up her laptop, ever since her arrival back home: she Googled 'Nico Cazale' and devoured every piece of information on him.

Kim, her virtual assistant, was on the line.

"Yes, you want *me* to go ahead and deal with all the queries or yes, *you'll look* into them?" Kim's voice was laced with irritation.

"Yes, I mean, *no*. I mean *you* deal with them, for now." Ava paused to examine a photo of Nico with yet another beautiful young thing. "I'm still busy uploading the ... images ... for the new products." It was an old picture, judging by Nico's boyish grin.

She threw down her damp cloth and sniffled into a Kleenex. The first few days of discovering all about Nico's love life had her in tears. Now the floodgates were under control, sort of.

"Have you got a cold?" Kim asked.

"No. I'm fine."

"It's just that you sound unwell."

"I'm fine."

"Okay, well, let me know if you need a hand with anything for the new products."

She knew what Kim was thinking but was too polite to say. *What the hell have you been doing for the past week?*

"I will. Thanks, Kim. Bye." Glad to have ended the call, Ava knew she could never afford to lose Kim. This woman was a super VA. She was indispensable. She'd been running Ava's online store just fine while Ava had been in Italy and now that she was back she really did need to get on with things. She'd sunk a ton of money into buying products from Italy and now she needed to make sure she sold them.

Or else there would be trouble.

Wiping her nose again, she clicked on the pictures on her screen. This man was so annoyingly handsome, and women were always draped around him. She knew these pictures well. Had stared at them for days.

She hated looking at them and yet she couldn't tear herself away from them either.

It had been seven days since she'd left Nico high and dry. Seven days she had spent moping around her apartment, except for the few times she had gone out to stock up on groceries.

Seven days where she had wondered whether she had been hasty in jumping to mile high conclusions and rushing back home.

Only the imminent arrival of her mom and sister tomorrow had propelled her into getting out today. She had hoped that cleaning up her mom's apartment, having a change of scenery, might motivate her into getting some actual work done, instead of endlessly and obsessively reading about the man who was out of her league.

The man who was also the father of the child she now carried. Something he had no knowledge of.

She touched her belly again, something she been doing a lot ever since she'd found out. She still had a few months to think things through; she was only around six weeks pregnant and the baby wasn't due until mid-November. Time was on her side.

Time to figure out what she was going to do.

In the cold light of day in Denver, away from the headiness of Verona, Venice, and Nico, she was aware of her haste in rushing back. Staring at the countless gossip column inches and photos of Nico and various beauties from his past, she had to wonder: what had he ever seen in her?

Finding him with that woman in his office had tipped her over the edge. She'd left Verona and flown back to Denver, leaving her mother and sister wondering what on earth had happened.

Now she was left wondering if she'd done the right thing.

Shouldn't she at least have given Nico the chance to explain himself? Could a man really be different things to different women?

The shock of her pregnancy and the sudden panic of being with a man she couldn't trust, who might hurt her again, had panicked her into fleeing. Nico had never even told her he loved her.

Maybe he didn't love her.

Maybe a man like Nico was incapable of loving anyone. And the only way he operated was by having many women at his beck and call.

Something about the air in Verona had made her throw caution to the wind, and the beauty of Venice had made her drunk on life and love. Her guard had come down, and she'd let Nico in. Somewhere, somehow, she had started to think that this jaw-droppingly handsome man would want her. She had made the mistake of allowing herself to believe it.

But even though she had tried to overlook his past and his reputation, believing he had changed, *her* doubts about herself never really disappeared. It wasn't just the woman in his office, or the women everywhere that he seemed to have dated at one time or another.

It was *her*.

Why would a man like Nico Cazale ever be interested in her?

The jeering voices from her past, from high-school, when she'd been labeled a freak, for being so tall and so thin, still screamed out at her at times when she felt vulnerable.

She got up, just to get away from the images on her screen and started wiping down the kitchen cabinets again. It was therapeutic. Being busy with housework kept her mind free from drifting.

Maybe she wasn't good enough. It wasn't just Nico who'd had a roving eye. In the end, even Connor had cheated on her.

She'd left Verona, knowing that she had only a short window of time to tell her mother of her last-minute decision to get the next flight out. It had been a freaky stroke of luck to get a seat the next morning. She'd flown back on the same flight as Connor, and he'd managed to get their seats so that they ended up sitting together. It was a small price to pay for escaping from her summer romance.

Surprisingly, Connor had left her alone during the flight. He hadn't asked any questions, but she knew he had them, especially after she'd asked him to hand back the Flamentagostini bracelet.

Ava wondered what Nico would have made of that. She hadn't thought it through when she'd given it to Connor. But now, according to her mom, Nico believed she'd gone back to Connor and *that* was her reason for absconding to Denver so quickly.

Finally finished with the cleaning, she collapsed into a chair and looked around the kitchen. She ran her hands over her flat belly. Hard to imagine that in eight months' time she would have another little person to take care of. It was something she had never considered, and it was so far off her radar that even now she had problems trying to get used to the fact that she was pregnant.

In the space of a year she'd gone from being almost married, to going on honeymoon alone, to now dealing with being pregnant.

Alone.

She moved her hand away from her belly; she would need to be extra careful around other people, especially her family, since she planned on keeping them in the dark for as long as possible, until she was used to this life-changing event herself.

She also planned on keeping Nico in the dark, until she figured out when she would tell him. Or whether she ever would.

If he ever found out that he was the father of her baby and that she had kept it from him, there would be hell to pay.

It would be another three months before anyone noticed

the weight gain. She wished she had paid more attention to her sister when she'd been pregnant, because Ava knew next to nothing about pregnancy.

Like most things in her life, she would have to learn as she went along. Her sickness wasn't too bad, just early morning for now. But come late summer, the news would no longer remain hidden.

And she had to make sure she worked hard during the next few months to ensure the success of her online store so that she would at least have some sort of income for them both; the baby and her.

She got her things together and got ready to leave. She had filled up her mom's refrigerator with milk, bread and a few other essentials, and had baked a small lasagna.

Carlos, her sister's husband, said he'd pick them up from the airport when they arrived later tomorrow night. Ava would visit her mother in a couple of days. She was in no hurry to confront her so soon. Not with her mother still looking for answers from her.

She would call Andrea tomorrow, feeling guilty because deep down inside, she was avoiding it.

Anything to do with Italy instantly reminded her of Nico, and she intended to forget that she had ever set eyes on him. Right or wrong, that was her plan, and she was sticking to it, for now.

HONEYMOON BLUES is available everywhere

BOOKLIST

Honeymoon Series: Take a roller-coaster journey of emotional highs and lows in this story of love and loss, family and relationships. When Ava is dumped six weeks before her Valentine's Day wedding, she has no idea of the life that awaits her in Italy.

Honeymoon for One
Honeymoon for Three
Honeymoon Blues
Honeymoon Bliss
Baby Steps
Honeymoon Series (Books 1-3)

Italian Summer Series: This is a spin-off from the Honeymoon Series. These books tell the stories of the secondary characters who first appeared in the Honeymoon Series. Nico and Ava also appear in these books.

It Takes Two
All That Glitters

Fool's Gold
Roman Encounter
November Sun
New Beginnings
Italian Summer Series (Books 1-4)

The Billionaire's Love Story: This is a Cinderella story with a touch of Jerry Maguire. What happens when the billionaire with too much money meets the single mom with too much heart?

<u>The Promise (FREE)</u>
The Gift, Book 1
The Gift, Book 2
The Gift, Book 3
The Gift, Boxed Set (Books 1, 2 & 3)
The Offer, Book 1
The Offer, Book 2
The Offer, Book 3
The Offer, Boxed Set (Books 1, 2 & 3)
The Vow, Book 1
The Vow, Book 2
The Vow, Book 3
The Vow, Boxed Set (Books 1, 2 & 3)

Indecent Intentions: This is a spin-off from The Billionaire's Love story. This 2-book set consists of 2 standalone stories about the billionaire's playboy brother. The 2nd story is about a wealthy nightclub owner who shuns relationships.

The Bet
The Hookup

Indecent Intentions 2-Book Set

The Seven Sins: A series of seven standalone romances based on the seven sins. Emotional, and angsty romances which are loosely connected.

Underdog (FREE prequel)
The Wrath of Eli
The Problem with Lust
The Lies of Pride
The Price of Inertia
The Other Side of Greed
The Seven Sins Books 1-3

A Perfect Match Series: This is a seven book series in which the first four books feature the same couple. High-flying corporate executive Nadine has no time for romance but her life takes a turn for the better when she meets Ethan, a sexy and struggling metal sculptor five years younger. He works as an escort in order to make the rent. Books 4-6 are standalone romances based on characters from the earlier books. The main couple, Ethan and Nadine, appear in all books:

Lost in Solo (prequel)
The Proposal
Heart Sync
A Leap of Faith
A Perfect Match Series Books 1-3
Misplaced Love
Reclaiming Love
Embracing Love
A Perfect Match Series (Books 4-6)

Standalone Books:

Tomorrow Belongs to Us
Love Among the Ruins
Love Inc
An Unexpected Gift

ABOUT THE AUTHOR

Lily Zante lives with her husband and three children somewhere near London, UK.

Connect with Me

I love hearing from you – so please don't be shy! Email me (lily@lilyzante.com), message me on Facebook or connect with me through these different platforms:

Instagram | Facebook | Twitter | Website

Follow me on Bookbub
Follow me on Goodreads
Follow me on TikTok
Join my FB Reader Group